Train to the Sun

2

Published by Airplane Books

Train to the Sun

Don Yarber

4

This book is dedicated to my wife,
Shirley Joye Yarber
for believing in me.

6

Thank you to:

Janis Rebecca for reading early drafts.

Thank you, Deborah Boydston, Leonard a. Wronke, Warren Gates, Leslie Blackwell and Jim Miller, all friends from ScribeSlice, for their recommendations and encouragement after the first four chapters.

Thanks to Buz Riley, WPR publishing, for technical advice regarding horseshoes and the farrier trade.

TRAIN TO THE SUN

The pack horse that carried Will suddenly slumped forward, tripped over its own front feet and fell hard. Fortunately for Will it hit on its right shoulder and then rolled, pinning Will's right foot and leg beneath it. Had it fell full force on its side first, it would have broken Will's leg.

I got my horse stopped and dismounted. When I looked, I saw immediately what the problem was. A rattler had attached itself to the packhorse's right front leg and was still hanging there like a leach. I put the heel of my boot on its head and ground it into the sand.

It took twenty minutes of sweating, grunting, heaving and cussing to get the horse off of Will's leg. The horse was still alive but breathing heavily, its breath rasping in and out of its chest, its right front forelock swollen to the size of a small tree. I hated to do it but I hauled out my Colt and shot the horse in the head, heaved Will up on the paint horse I had been riding, and tied him on.

Will's body lay heavy in the saddle in front of me. He was still alive, although barely. His breathing had almost stopped and when I put my ear to his chest I could barely hear his heart beat. I had ridden fifty miles with him across the saddle, me sitting behind the cantle, pushing the gelded paint as hard as I dared. If it threw a shoe, stepped in a gopher hole, or shied at a rattler, there would be two dead men on the trail. When we left our place Will was riding a pack horse, now that horse was dead, and Will was dying.

The only chance to save Will's life was the railroad. The train could reach the doctor in Tucson in a day where it would take us two weeks on the tired and thirsty paint horse. After riding all day, I finally saw the tracks ahead of me and wondered if I had reached them in time. The train traveled every week through this spot in the desert. It passed this point at about the same time. right about the time the sun cast the shadows from the telegraph poles long enough to reach the track on the near side. I pulled my Granddad's watch from my pocket and saw that it was nearly 5:30. Another hour and the train would be rumbling through, I'd made it on time.

I dismounted in the shade of two saguaro, stomped around them to scare any rambling rattlesnakes away from the spot, then eased Will's thin body down till his boots hit the ground. I got around on that side and lifted his bound wrists over the saddle horn and caught him under the arms and laid him as gently as I could in the shade of the cactus.

The paint sidled away from me sideways and I had to take two quick steps to catch the reins and ease him back. He didn't like the looks of the body on the ground but he was grateful, for the moment, that he wasn't carrying two people.

"Stand still, Paint," I said.

I threw the reins over an arm of the saguaro and Paint stood still. I took the canteen from the saddle horn and kneeling beside Will, raised his head with one hand and touched the canteen to his lips with the other. He opened his eyes for a brief second and smiled at me. His eyes said thank you and then closed again as he swallowed two or three sips of water, then he was off to never-never land again, somewhere between hell and heaven, half alive, half dead.

I put his hat over his face to keep the flies and the sun off of it, stood and pulled the makings out of my shirt pocket, rolled one and dug in filthy denims for a match. I found one and flicked it to life with my thumb nail and touched the flame to the roll-your-own cigarette. I took a deep drag and let the smoke trickle out slow. It might be the last one I could smoke before I put Will on the train, then the long ride on in to Tucson. I'd get there with enough supplies, I was pretty sure, but getting Will there was the important thing.

It wasn't long before I could feel the train coming. First you feel the vibrations in the sand, like a million half starved longhorns stampeding to a water hole, or a million scorpions slithering under your feet. Then you hear the wind whistling past the cattle guards, then the clickety clack of the wheels. I mounted and rode towards the oncoming train pulling a red bandana off of my neck as I rode. Five hundred yards away I reined to a halt and put Paint in the middle of the tracks and started waving the bandana. A single blast on the whistle told me that someone on board had seen me, then I could hear the sound of the wheels diminish slightly, a giant hiss of steam escaping, then metal on metal as brakes were applied. I sat transfixed on the back of my horse as the train got closer and closer.

When it was a mere twenty yards away, I raked spurs across Paint's flanks and he lurched off of the track.

I jerked the reins up fifteen feet on the other side of the tracks and wheeled the horse's head to face the train as it raced by, squealing brakes, metal wheels sliding on metal track. It finally screeched to a stop nearly a quarter of a mile from where I sat. I spurred the horse into a gallop and rode towards the engine. A man swung down from the open engine door onto a step and waited.

When I was close enough I yelled at him.

"Thanks for stopping," I said.

"What's the problem?"

"I've got a sick man I need to get to Tucson."

"You'll have to talk to Chester about that," he told me.

"Who's Chester, and where do I find him?"

"He'd be that fat fart coming down the middle of the train about now," the engineer said.

I glanced up towards the aisle running through the cars. There were only two passenger cars a freight car and the engine and the caboose. A heavy man wearing dark blue pants and shirt and a funny looking hat with a silver badge on it waddled toward me.

"Are you Chester?" I asked.

"That is correct. I'm Chester Peak. What can I do for you?"

"My pardner is back about a eighth of a mile. He's deathly ill and needs to get to Tucson to a doc."

"Well, does he have the fare?" Chester asked.

"How much of a fare does a dying man need?" I asked.

"Same as a living one, stranger," Chester said. "No free rides on this train, I'd lose my job bigger'n shit."

"How much of a fare?"

"Twenty dollars ought to cover it," he said, grinning. I didn't see anything funny about it.

Twenty dollars was about five times more than I thought it should be.

"Twenty dollars? I've barely got ten. "Can you bill me for the other ten?"

I had stuffed a twenty dollar bill in Will's right boot and a note in his shirt pocket for the doctor, telling him where to find the money for Will's treatment. I didn't want this fat, greedy man to know that, however.

"This isn't a charity train, it's a cash and carry, Mister. It's twenty dollars or your friend can walk to Tucson and find his own doctor."

I thought fast. I had to get Will on this train. I knew he'd die if he didn't get medical treatment. Everything I'd tried had only postponed the inevitable. Will's insides were poisoning him and no matter what I did, he was getting worse.

I hauled out my Grandfather's gold watch.

"I've got this watch. It ought to be worth $10."

"Lemme see it," Chester Peak said.

I handed it to him. He turned it over and over like it was a diamond, handling it carefully.

"Put him on board, stranger. You've bought him a ride."

"Will you get him in the hands of a doctor in Tucson?"

"I'll take care of it." Chester told me. I had no reason to doubt him, and had to trust him. He was my only hope to save Will's life.

I put my left foot in the stirrup and swung up on Paint and galloped back to where I had left Will. He didn't wake up when I picked him up and propped him against Paint. I grabbed him around his thighs and heaved till he was stretched over the saddle again. I walked behind Paint and put my hands on his butt and vaulted up behind the saddle, reaching over Will to take the reins. I jerked and spun Paint towards the train and galloped back.

The fat conductor didn't offer to help and it was about all I could do to get Will off of Paint, up the stairs and onto the train. I got him to a passenger car and laid him down across an empty seat.

"Don't worry, Will," I said, even though I knew he was unconscious. "This train will get you to Tucson and there's a doctor there. He'll take good care of you. I'll follow the train and see you soon."

The train started inching ahead. I had just enough time to get off and grab Paint's reins before the train lumbered off, clickety clacking once again on the steel rails headed towards the setting sun.

CHAPTER 2

I rode easy, following the tracks of the railroad. I had water enough for a week, if I was careful, but I knew that the tracks would lead me to water. Trains can't live without water any more than man can. Somewhere along the way they would have to take on water. Wherever that happened to be, I'd fill up my water jugs too. Food? That was a different story. Trains eat wood. I couldn't.

Long after dark I decided I'd ridden Paint about as far as he was willing to go that day so I stopped and built a small fire out of mesquite brush and dried cactus. I put on a pot and boiled water for coffee, cut a piece of jerky and ate it and drank a cup of hot bitter coffee. I threw Paint's reins over his head and just for safety sake tied a rope around his right front leg and around my waist. He wouldn't wonder far without waking me up. I took off my belt and let the holstered Colt 44 slide down easy, rolled the belt around the holster and stuck it under the saddle that I used for a pillow, and laid myself down on half of the saddle blanket and pulled the other half over me. It gets cold at night in the desert.

I listened to the distant sound of a coyote, yipping at the moon, singing me a lullaby. It didn't take me long, tired as I was, to fall into that bottomless pit of sleep. I didn't dream. Seems like I don't dream much anymore. Used to dream all the time. Women, whiskey, poker games, dances, music, all were part of my dreams. Two years of trying to scratch out a living on the northern edge of this damned desert had killed the dreaming.

Will and I had ventured west after the war. Neither of us had relatives that we cared enough about to go back to. Will was an orphan who had been raised by a one armed man. The man had lost his arm in the war of 1812 and was still cussing the British.

My Momma was Chickasaw and Pa was Irish. They had died of smallpox. Ma got it first, then pa. Both of them died within a week. I don't know why I didn't get it. I dug graves for them both and was throwing the dirt in on them when a bunch of rebel soldiers rode by. One asked me what happened and I told him. He gave me a potato and a cracker and told me I'd starve if I stayed there, might as well join up with them.

I took to him right away. His name was Will and he'd only been a soldier for a month. He said the food was OK and he wasn't getting beat by a one armed man any more so he reckoned he'd be a soldier. Will was a year older than me, and at 15, a little taller, although I probably outweighed him by a few pounds. We made a good team, both of us were good riders and we were assigned to a Major as messengers.

Our company was caught off guard by a much larger force of Yankees one night and Will and I got separated. When he found me I'd been shot through the upper right leg and he bandaged me up and helped me get on his horse. He rode with me half the night till we caught up with the fast retreating company. They left me at a hospital in Alabama and Will deserted to stay nearby. After a while they discharged me and Will and I headed back towards my home in Kentucky. A few nights into the ride we got word that the war was over. The Yanks had won.

I don't remember when we decided to go west, it was probably in the summer of 1868 or 69. I know we should have stayed in Kentucky. The journey west was one of disappointment and difficulties. Half of our wagon train didn't make it as far as Oklahoma and about that time Will told me he wanted to try to go as far as California. He said there was free land there and we could start a ranch together.

We never made it.

We worked for a man in Abilene long enough to buy twenty head of cattle and a bull. Our horses were the same ones we had ridden during the war. They were stout and capable. It was the two of us who weren't so stout.

Two hundred miles north and east of Tucson is as far as we got.

We'd built a cabin, expanded our heard to about 30 head, worked ourselves to the bone, and lived on antelope and corn pone. The land we had decided to try to start our ranch on was free. Hell, it should have been. Rattlesnakes and coyotes are about all that could live there. We were on the northern edge of the Sonoma desert. We found a fresh water spring and dug it deep enough so we could water the stock. We planted corn, potatoes, and tobacco. Very little of it survived in the sandy soil. We learned to make a flat dry bread out of cornmeal and water. An Indian showed us how to do that.

So we weren't desperate, but we weren't getting rich either.

Then Will got sick.

I'd heard of appendix while in the hospital and all of his symptoms pointed to appendix poisoning. I wanted to get him to a doctor right away but he said he'd be OK and that it was just the damned food. But he didn't get OK.

Now he was on a train headed for Tucson and I was just drifting off to sleep next to a bed of railroad tracks where the only other living things within two hundred miles were scorpions, coyotes, rattlesnakes and buzzards.

CHAPTER 3

I was up with the sun the next morning, stiff and cold. It was still cold. I could see Paint's breath as we rode towards Tucson, following the railroad tracks. By noon it had not only warmed up a bit but got danged hot. Sweat was running down my forehead, stinging my eyeballs. I'd say it was near to ninety. When we reached a water tank I dismounted and headed Paint for the shade.

The sun was straight overhead and it was hard to see anything in the shade of the water tank. When I got close enough, there seemed to be a dark shape laying in the shade. I thought at first that a wayward stranger was sleeping under the tank, waiting for the next train. I was wrong.

It was Will.

I knew he was dead before I got within twenty feet of him. I could smell the death all around him. A coyote sprinted ten yards away, out into the bright sun, dragging something behind it. A single buzzard was circling high overhead.

I drew the .44 and shot the coyote. Then I pointed the gun up at the buzzard and fired again. I missed it but the sound of the gun made it sail off towards a cactus a few hundred feet away where it landed. I pulled my Winchester out of the saddle holster and shot its head off.

I stepped the final few feet to the body.

The coyote had gnawed through Will's stomach wall and the stench of rotting gut enveloped me. It was part of Will's intestines that the coyote had been dragging.

The sadness and depression fell on me like rain. I hadn't had time to grieve much when my mom and pop died, and I wouldn't have much time to grieve now, but I stood silently sobbing for several minutes.

Will's dead. Why?

What was the reason that Chester Peak had left Will's body here, why didn't he take it on in to Tucson for a proper burial?

I knelt beside Will and picked up his hands and folded them over his chest. That's when I saw that he'd been shot. There was a hole in his chest. Why would anyone shoot him? He might have lived if he'd reached a doctor in time. Then I noticed Will's boots were gone. So was the note I'd left in his shirt pocket. So was the twenty dollars I'd put in his right boot.

I gathered rocks from around the water tower and piled them on Will. It took me the rest of the day and it was almost dark when I put the final rock on the grave and stopped to say goodbye to my friend. I was crying when I knelt beside his grave.

"So long, Will," I told him. "I don't know who did this. I swear to you though, I'll find out. Whoever did this aint going to live long."

I filled my water jugs and rode away.

* * * * * * * *

Thirteen days later I rode in to Tucson. I was so tired I couldn't think straight. I'd gone without water the last two days and my mouth felt like it had chewed on a green persimmon. My lips were cracked and I had a layer of dust on my face an inch thick. My hair was caked with dried dirt and sweat. The sombrero I wore was floppy and ragged around the edges but it was the only one I owned. The denims were so stiff from dirt and sweat that I felt they might walk away on their own if I could step out of them. My boot soles were getting so thin I figured I could read a newspaper through them.

Paint made his way to a livery, smelling water and food. I stayed on him until he got under the livery roof, then I tried to get off and couldn't get my left foot out of the stirrup so I fell off. Paint took two steps and stopped. A grisly looking old blacksmith helped me get my foot out of the stirrup and got me to me feet.

"You need a drink, young feller," he said.

"Water," was all I could say.

He fetched a dipper full of brackish tasting water and I drank it down, thankful for it. I held the dipper up for more and he shook his head.

"No. You drink another dipper full and you'd be sick as a dog."

"Thank you," I told him.

"How long you been riding?"

"Seems like a month," I said through parched lips. "Three days from my spread to the railroad and fourteen days from there to here."

"Why didn't you take the train?"

"Money," I said. "I put my sick pardner on the train. paid $10 and my gold watch for his fare. Next day I found him under a water tank. He'd been shot."

"Shot?"

"Yes sir. I'm here to see if I can find a railroad conductor by the name of Chester Peak. He might know who shot Will."

"Will was your pardner? Was he shot before or after you put him on the train?"

"After," I said. "He was suffering from appendix poison. I paid Chester Peak the money and the watch to get Will here to a doctor. That train passed me going east yesterday. I don't know if Peak was on it, but I'll wait till it comes back through here again."

"Won't be back through here for another two weeks, cowboy," the blacksmith said. "You won't last two weeks if you don't get some grub in you."

"I've been eating," I said. "I boiled some cactus and ate it yesterday, had a cup of coffee to wash it down with."

"Come with me, young feller," the smithy said. "I'll buy you a meal. You can work it off mucking the livery stables for me."

I followed him through the livery and out a back door onto a narrow dirt street, lined on both sides by wooden side walks. He turned right and I fell in behind him until he stopped and waited for me to catch up.

"Before I take you in the hotel for a meal, I'd better get you cleaned up a bit. You smell like you've already been mucking stables for two weeks."

"I don't doubt that," I said. "Aint had a bath in two months. It's hard to stay clean when you work thirty head of cattle and take care of a sick man, do all the cooking and plantin' by yourself."

"Well they's baths for a nickel. You got any clean clothes?"

"A shirt. These denims are the only britches I own."

"Lord a mercy," the blacksmith said. "Well, get in there and get a bath. I'll be back with a pair of britches that might come close to fittin, and I'll fetch your shirt."

He gave me a nickel and pointed towards the hotel door. I walked in and asked for a bath. The clerk looked at me like she wanted to puke, pointed to a room on the far side of the hotel and handed me a towel.

"That'll be five cents. The tub's in there and there's water in it. You'll find soap on the floor next to the tub. No smoking while you're soaking. If I smell smoke in there you'd best be on fire."

I gave her the nickel and smiled at her.

"I promise I won't smoke in the tub," I said.

The water in the tub looked like someone else had already bathed in it, but I wasn't in any shape or mood to argue about it. I stripped and got in it. Surprisingly the water was hot. I sat down in the tub and leaned back and relaxed. I wanted a smoke so bad I could have smoked the towel, but figured that I'd best wait.

I guess I fell asleep. I woke up when I heard water pouring into the tub. I looked up and saw the clerk with a kettle of steaming water, pouring it into the tub. She glanced at my naked body while she was pouring and turned rapidly away, but not before I caught a glimpse of a half smile on her face. I didn't know if that meant she was pleased with what she had seen or was laughing at it. She walked back out and closed the door behind her.

I fished the bar of soap off of the floor and started scrubbing. When I felt I'd scrubbed a boxcar full of dirt off of my arms and legs and torso, I let myself slide until my head went under water, then came back up and rubbed the soap bar in my hair. Twenty minutes later I stood up and climbed out of the tub, rubbing my aching bones with the rough towel. The blacksmith had returned with the shirt out of my saddle bags and a pair of britches that fit me better than the stinking denims I had removed. I put the clean clothes on and dunked my dirty socks in the tub and washed them with the bar of soap. I wrung them nearly dry and pulled them back on my aching feet. The cool socks felt good to my toes. I picked up my boots and carried them under my arm back into the hotel lobby. My new friend, the blacksmith, was waiting for me.

"You feel better now?" he asked.

"Almost like a human being," I said.

"Get some grub in you. You'll live," he said, grinning.

We went through a double door into a dining room. The long table was crowded with men, all of them poking food into their faces like there wasn't going to be a tomorrow. We found seats across from each other and sat down. The same clerk that had poured water on my naked body brought a bowl of beans and a platter of fried pork and sat it in front of us. I ladled beans onto the pewter plate in front of me and picked up a spoon and started eating.

"My name is Dewey Bradshaw," my friend told me. "What's yours?"

"Charles Merritt," I said. "Charles Martin Merritt the Third."

"Who was the first two?" he asked.

"Well, my Pa was one of them," I said. "I guess Grandpa was the other one."

He picked up the platter of pork and slid two large chunks onto his plate then handed the platter to me.

"Get some of this meat," he said. "You need to eat if you're gonna work for me."

I ate.

CHAPTER 4

I didn't mind working for Dewey Bradshaw. He was a kind man, a church go-er and a gentleman. His business was the only one within miles and he did quite well. Shoeing horses is an art and Old Dewey agreed to shoe Paint. Paint needed new shoes almost as bad as I did. When Dewey offered me a pair of boots that he'd taken from a dead man I was deeply grateful. They fit like they were made for me. I learned later that the britches he'd given me were from the same corpse.

A gambler had won a considerable poke at the saloon and a wild cowboy didn't take kindly to being stripped of a month's salary. He told the gambler that he didn't like being cheated. The gambler played his cards right. He told the cowboy to take it up with the proprietor. The cowboy said he was taking it up with the gambler, and drew down on him. The gambler shot the cowboy through the head with a little derringer pistol that he carried up his sleeve. The cowboy had just bought new britches and boots. Now I was wearing them.

"How'd you happen to get these britches from the saloon keeper?" I asked him one day.

"Well I'm the undertaker in this here town as well as the livery owner. I just helped myself."

Nevertheless I was grateful for them, and at the end of the week when he paid me seven dollars I offered to pay him for the clothes.

"No. Them's a gift. Just give me two dollars. That'll pay for your food this week and the nickel I gave you for the bath," he said. "Next week you can pay me for that Paint's food."

"I'm much obliged," I told him. "After that train comes in and I take care of my business with the conductor, I'm headed back to my spread in the northern Sonoma."

"Well, that's your business," he said. "I could use a hand like you, one that aint afraid of work."

The train pulled in to Tucson at the end of that week and I went looking for the conductor. He wasn't with the train. Instead, there was a small black man wearing the same kind of blue pants and shirt and wearing the funny hat with a silver badge on it. I asked him where Chester Peak was and he told me that Chester's missus was having a baby and that the fat man was taking a week off. He wouldn't be back on this train for another two weeks. I felt cheated.

Things would soon get real sorry if I didn't get back to my spread. Calves would be born and coyotes might eat them. The herd might get into the garden and eat every damned stalk of corn I'd planted. Hell the spring might dry up and all of them might die of starvation. I had to get back soon.

I found the engineer and asked him if he saw anyone get off the train when it stopped to take on water the day I put Will aboard.

"Yes, I did," he told me. "A man got off, half staggering. It was that young feller you brought. He was on the far side of the water tank and I was on the other side filling the boilers. I heard what sounded like a gun, but didn't pay much attention. People are always shooting at coyotes and critters from the train. Sometimes they shoot buffalo just to be shooting them. Never could see no sport in that."

"No, Sir." I said.

"So you didn't actually see anyone shoot Will?" I asked him.

"Was he shot? I know he didn't get back on the train, when we got to Tucson I saw Chester get off and go to the saloon. I thought he was going for the doctor. He came back by his self and no doctor ever came that I know of. I walked back to that car where you left that youngun and he was gone."

"Will never made it to Tucson," I said. "I found his body under the water tank. He'd been shot."

"That don't mean Chester shot him, son," the engineer said.

"Wouldn't he have tried to get him to a doctor?"

"Not if a customer complained about the smell," I was told. "Chester is a namby-pamby. He bends over and sticks his head up his ass to please riders, especially those he thinks will give him a dollar at the end of their ride."

"So you're telling me that Will might have got shot on the train?"

"I'm just speculatin' as to what might have happened."

"Well, thank you for your time," I told him.

I got aboard the train and walked to the car where I'd put Will. The seat I'd laid him on looked the same as it did before I put him on it. No blood stains. There were not any stains on the floor either. I didn't see any blood stains anywhere. Will was not shot on the train, I'd bet on it.

Later that day I told Dewey I was leaving.

"I'm riding back to my spread, Dewey." I said. "I can't wait here forever to ask questions of that conductor. If he shot Will, I'll find out someday, and when I do, I'll kill the son of a bitch."

"Don't blame you for being bitter, son," Dewey said. "But vengeance belongs only to the Lord. You'd be better off just forgetting that conductor. If that spread of your'n don't work out, come back. I'll put you to work."

"I don't think the Lord meant me to muck stables for the rest of my life, Dewey," I said. "The only thing I know how to do is ride. Been riding since I was big enough to walk."

"Well the Sheriff needs a deputy here. Maybe he'd hire you. If you was a law man you'd be in a better position to bring Will's killer to justice the legal way."

"Vengeance may be the Lord's" I told him. "Will's killer is mine. When I find him there won't be any justice more than he gave Will."

"In that case, son, be smart. If you get on that train and you shoot that conductor, the law will be after you. I can't say as I'd blame you if you shoot Will's killer, but think of what the law will do to you. They'd track you down and hang you, son."

"Maybe." I said.

"Well at least when you get on the train, pull a bandana over your face so people won't remember your face. They can't identify a man in court whose face they've never seen. Might keep you from hangin' someday."

"Thanks, Dewey. I'll remember that. I'll be back someday, and when I come back I'll pay you for all I owe you. And thank you for helping me. I don't think I could have made it through these past two weeks without you."

"You'd a made it, son. You're the kind that will make it no matter what the difficulty is. You are honest and hard working. That makes you a good man in my eyes. Good luck to you, Charles Merritt. May God bless you."

He gave me a two week supply of hardtack and beans, a chunk of jerky and some coffee. He insisted on giving me a box of 44's and some 44-40's. I told him I'd pay him next time I saw him.

"I'll be leaving early," I said. "So goodbye, Dewey Bradshaw. Thank ye."

We shook hands and I climbed up in the barn loft at the livery, stretched out on a pile of hay and put everything out of my mind except the trip ahead of me and finding Will's killer. It was nearly midnight when I drifted off to sleep.

CHAPTER 5

Next morning I was on the trail before sunup. The trail out of Tucson was wide for the first couple of miles, then narrowed a bit, as it went east and followed the railroad, then eventually it was just the track. Mile after mile of twelve by twelve by eight foot railroad ties, spaced evenly apart, steel rails spiked to the ties. The morning sun reflected off of the steel no matter which way I faced east. I pulled my dirty old hat down over my eyes, gave Paint his head and rode easy in the saddle, dozing most of the time.

I dreamed in short spurts about Will. Will and I working together, straining hard on barbed wire, digging through sand and rock to set fence posts, shoveling for days to make a watering hole, eating meager rations and hoping our herd would expand enough to make it through the next season.

During my woke up hours I thought about what I was going to do. I realized that without help I probably would not be able to maintain the spread. Best thing to do, I thought, would be to round up the herd, drive them to the nearest ranch, and sell them for whatever I could get. Then pack up my meager possessions and move back to Tucson, maybe take that job as deputy.

The idea of finding Will's killer kept haunting me.

I made better time going back than I had riding towards Tucson after finding Will's body. I had more supplies, more water and was rested. Paint was rested too, and we made it back to the water tank in ten days. I stopped and dismounted next to the pile of rocks, sat down on them, took off my hat and poured a little water on my bandana to cool my face. That's why it happened that I had my bandana in my hand when I heard the train. It was a long way off yet, but I could feel it. I walked to the track, holding on to Paint's reins, knelt and put my ear to a rail. I cold hear the steady rumbling sound coming through the steel. My guess was the train was five miles out. I got on Paint and rode a short way out through the sand, found a place where the wind had piled up a dune and rode behind it.

I pulled the Colt and examined it. It was fully loaded. I pulled the bandana up over my face and tied the knot securely behind my neck and waited.

When the train stopped and the engineer got out to refill the water tank I rode fast to the first car and swung off of Paint onto the steps, holding the rail. I tied Paint to the rail and walked down the aisle of the cars, Colt in my right hand. I found Chester Peak in the second car.

"Why'd you shoot Will?" I asked him through the bandana.

"What? Who are you? I didn't shoot anyone!" he said, adamantly.

"You know who I am, and you know who Will was. He's buried out there under that pile of rocks. I want to know why you robbed him and shot him, you're gonna tell me, then I'm going to put a bullet in your fat gut and let you die like you let Will die."

"Now, nn..nn.now hold on there…"

"Start talking!"

"You…you're the man who brought that sick man on the train!"

"And you're the one who shot him," I said.

"Now wait just a minute," Chester said, sweat popping out suddenly on his face. "I remember you. But I didn't shoot your friend."

"If you didn't, who did?" I asked grabbing his shirt collar and pulling him closer, the barrel of the .44 against his chest.

He moved as if trying to get away but my grip on his collar was too tight. He gagged a bit, then tried to speak, gagging again. I let up on my hold so he could talk.

"Spit it out," I told him.

"There was another feller in this car," he finally said, still coughing.

"And?"

"I found the note in your friend's pocket. I read it and put it back," he said. "I got to feeling guilty about your grandpa's watch so I stuck that in his pocket too."

"Then you took him off of the train, under the water tank and put a bullet in his chest."

"No....no..I didn't do that!"

"Who did?"

"I believe it was the other feller who was sitting there!" Chester pointed across the aisle to the seat opposite where I'd left Will. I vaguely remembered a tall thin man in a dapper outfit sitting there. The man had worn a fancy revolver on a tool engraved belt under his vest. I remembered the grips on his pistol, they were silver.

"So did you see that feller shoot Will?"

"I didn't see him, but he must have been the one who did it," Chester said.

"What did you see?"

"I left your friend there in the seat," Chester told me. "When I came back he was gone. The other feller was gone, too. I returned to the caboose, looking in all the cars for your friend. He wasn't on board. Then I saw the fancy dude get on right behind the engine. That was just as the train started to move again."

"Did you ask him about Will?"

"I said, 'do you know where that man is that was sitting here?' and he gave me a nasty look and said, 'it aint my day to watch your passengers, fat man' so I went on about my business."

"Are you telling me the truth, Chester Peak? Cause if I find you lied to me, I'll find you again. I swear I'll beat you half to death and shoot you the rest of the way!"

"I...I..I'm telling you the truth!" he said. "I've got a wife and a new son back in Cleveland. I swear I'm not lying to you!"

I let go off his shirt and spun on my heel. The train was starting to move again, slow. I walked towards the handrail where I had tied Paint. As I passed through the next car I glanced to my left and saw a man standing there. He had on a pair of blue pants like Chester Peak's, a white shirt and a blue vest. His hat was similar to Chester's but without a badge.

In his hand was a large canvas bag, he extended it towards me.

"Take it, Mister." He said. "Take it, but please don't shoot me. I'm new on this job, and I aint armed."

I could tell he was nervous from the sound of his voice. What puzzled me was why he was trying to give me a canvas bag. The train lurched just at that point and he dropped the bag at my feet. Instinctively, I picked it up. Thinking that the train was moving a little faster, I hurried towards the spot where Paint was tied. By now the train had picked up considerable speed. Paint was trotting at a fast pace to keep up, the reins tied to the rail. I untied them and shoved the Colt in my holster, grabbed the saddle horn and swung out and over, landing in the saddle, my right hand still holding the canvas bag.

I raked spurs across Paint's haunches and neck reined him hard right. He jumped and his forefeet slid a little as he landed in sand and rock on the track bed. Then he bolted and we were speeding off at a fast gallop away from the train. I heard shouts behind me, then the sound of gunfire.

It didn't occur to me that anyone would be shooting at me.

When a slug zipped close enough to my ear to sound like a mad bumble bee, I slapped the reins between Paint's ears and he turned it up a notch. We were soon far enough away that the shouts and shots were faint and far behind us.

As sure as I'm telling you this, I still hadn't considered what was in the bag or why I was being shot at.

It was only when I reached my dilapidated shack a day later that I opened the bag and found the money. I counted it and there was nearly $3000 in cash. Slowly, like stink off of a horse apple, it dawned on me. *I had robbed the train.* I hadn't meant to rob any one, let alone a train. But nevertheless, as I stood there with both hands full of cash, I realized that I had, indeed, robbed the train. That man in the funny blue suit must have been the railroad paymaster, taking money to Tucson to be transferred west for payroll.

No wonder they were shooting at me. I was a highwayman. A rail rod. A bandito. Me? I'd never stolen a thing in my life and hadn't intended to this time. But I was a thief, never-the-less. Train robber! I thought about what Dewey Bradshaw had told me about wearing a mask. If I'd *NOT* been wearing that danged bandana around my face, the paymaster wouldn't have handed over that bag of money.

Well, there was just one thing to do. Take it back.

But I had a lot of work to do before hand. Now I had no choice. I rounded up as much of the herd as I could find, packed some grub and water, and slowly looked around the place before I climbed on Paint and swung a rope and let out a yippee-cay-yee. The herd started moving slowly at first then trotted a few hundred feet before settling down and following a longhorn steer towards the nearest ranch which was nearly twenty miles away, along the Gila river bed. If I could get ten dollars a head for the twenty or so I was driving, I'd be happy. I realized that isn't what Will would have wanted me to do, but then Will's dead. I had to think of myself, and somehow find a way out of being a hold up man, train robber, and bandito. And, too, I wanted to find the dirty pole-cat that killed Will.

CHAPTER 6

With nearly $3000 stuffed in my saddle bags, I argued for fifteen minutes over fifty cents. My neighbor, Randolph Flockman was a hard man to bargain with. He offered me eight-fifty a head and I argued for nine. We cussed each other, called each other highway robbers (although I knew that I was one, and he wasn't), then I finally agreed to take the eight-fifty. We drove the small herd through a gate and his foreman counted them. I had nineteen steers and a half-grown calf. I knew there were ten or more head still on my place, but I didn't have the time to round them up.

Randy gave me a hundred and seventy dollars. I filled up my canteen from the cool water of the Gila and headed south, just me and Paint and $3170 in cash. I took the danged red bandana and tied it to Randy's barbed wire fence before I left.

"Hey, Charlie, you're leaving your bandana!" He yelled.

"Keep it, Randy," I yelled back. "Something to remember me by!"

I was dirty and my mouth was dry from eating trail dust all day, but I turned down an offer to spend the night at Randy's bunkhouse. I didn't want any of his hired hands to remember me and could do without any prying around my saddlebags. I wanted to return every penny I had stolen from the railroad, and anyone who found three thousand dollars might help themselves to a twenty or two.

So I rode out, headed south again. It had taken Will and I two days to make the trip from our little place to the railroad, but then Will was sick and I was taking it as easy as I could on him. Now I was twenty miles north of our spread, a day's ride away, and so it would take me at least two days to reach the tracks. I wished that I had my grandfather's watch so I could make sure I didn't miss that train. I wondered how much they would charge me to put Paint on the train. I wasn't even sure they allowed horses. Whatever it was, I'd pay it out of the $170 I got for my steers. The $3000 would go back to whoever on that train would take it and give me a written receipt for it.

Of all the times for it to rain in the desert, it rained on me and Paint that night. We had stopped at sundown in a hollow, a hundred feet across and four feet deep. I'd built a small fire, warmed some beans and made coffee. Paint had his supper of a double handful of oats and some grass from a half of a bale I'd bought from Randy.

I was so wore out that I didn't even feel the raindrops hitting my face. Old Paint whinnied and I woke up. My saddlebags were floating in a foot of water nearby. I grabbed them first thing, then the blanket. I pulled on my wet boots and threw the blanket on the horse. Paint didn't like the feel of a heavy, wet blanket, and sidled away from me. I had to whisper to him and then hold the reins with my left hand and hoist the wet saddle with my right. When I had it on and cinched down good, I tied the saddle bags to the cantle with a piece of rawhide and swung up into the saddle. Paint splashed his way to a high spot, climbed out of the hollow and stopped. Ahead of me water was running everywhere. There were little gullies and draws and washes all over the place, water running swiftly through them. Momentarily I was confused as to which way was South, the skies were dark. No stars to guide me. The tracks I'd made riding into the hollow spot would be gone by now, washed away by the rain. How the hell was I supposed to ride south when I didn't know which way south was?

I held Paint at a stop, the raindrops stinging my face. I cussed nature and everything about it. Here it is pouring down rain in the one spot where it only rains about twice a year, and then in the middle of the winter. This was spring, April or late March, I didn't know which, I'd lost all count of days.

One thing was sure, and that was my immediate need to get to higher ground. Deserts can be treacherous in a rainstorm. Places where you'd never worry about drowning can sweep you off of your feet and bury you in loose sand and water before you can say rattlesnake. I waited for a streak of lightning, and while the sky was partially lit, glanced around hurriedly and caught sight of a bluff to my left. I pointed Paint's nose in that direction and prodded him gently, letting him pick his way through the wet sand and water. Eventually we started a gentle climb up a slope and got out of the water danger. Half way up the slope the rocks rose straight into the night sky.

I found an overhanging rock and got under it, pulling the reins until I convinced Paint that he ought to join me under there. The roof over our heads was not much more than three inches above my head; it projected out about fifteen feet and the ground we stood on was level for ten feet before it tapered off sharply towards the spot from whence we had came.

I edged my way back under the overhang as far as I could get, hoping I didn't disturb a sleeping rattler or puma. Scorpions and Gila monsters are bad enough, but a rattlesnake or puma will kill a man faster. I wasn't anxious to make friends with any of them.

I kicked around till I was pretty sure I'd scared the critters away, then laid my aching bones down in the sand and tried to sleep. It wasn't cold, but being soaked to the bone was uncomfortable and I slept fitfully.

CHAPTER 7

I woke up with the weird sensation that someone was kicking my feet. It wasn't daylight yet, but the eastern sun was just cracking the horizon and when I opened my eyes I saw the silhouette of a man standing above me. At first I thought I was dreaming. Then I thought Will's ghost had come back to haunt me.

The rain had stopped. I lay there with my eyes not quite open, just squinted, almost afraid to open them all the way, waiting for Will to say something to me, like 'welcome to hell' or 'being dead aint so bad' was more like what Will might say.

Instead I heard nothing but the distant bark of a prairie dog.

I opened my eyes full wide. The man standing looking down at me was an Indian. He wasn't holding a knife or a gun or bow. I'd heard that a renegade bunch of Apaches were on the warpath in these parts, and I expected at any second that this Indian would pounce on my weary bones and stick a knife in my belly. I moved my right hand towards the spot I'd left the Colt, under the saddle.

"Why you here?"

Now that was a crazy question, I thought. I was there to get out of the rain.

"Rain," I said. "Damned near drowned."

"You go," he said, pointing out away from the rock outcrop that I had slept under.

"I go south. Which way?" I said.

"South?"

"Railroad. Iron horse. Which way?"

"Oh, south. That way," he pointed straight out in the direction I was facing. "You go to railroad?"

"Yes railroad."

This conversation was getting nowhere.

"Me too."

Great. A redskin to ride with. What else could befall me? I didn't need a guide, just point me south and I'll ride.

"What you called?" He asked.

"Charlie."

"Me name Skinny Horse."

"Howdy," I said.

"Howdy."

"We ride?" I asked him.

"Ride." He turned and walked out from under the overhang and I saw a small horse standing behind him. I hadn't seen it before since he had blocked my vision and it wasn't quite daylight. Now I could see it plain. It didn't have a saddle, just a leather hackamore.

I got up and stretched, yawning loudly. I pulled the saddle towards Paint and swung it up, cinched it and turned and picked up my belt with the holstered Colt. I strapped it on and led Paint out of my temporary shelter. Outside I glanced around expecting to see a thousand redskins in war paint. There were none.

Where the hell did he go? I looked all around me. Maybe he had been a ghost. Then I heard the soft sound of his pony's feet slapping the sand and swung into the saddle and urged Paint towards the sound. His pony had dropped into a gully ten feet deep and I looked for a way down that wouldn't jar my bones. I found a little cut in the bank and reined Paint down it. At the bottom I prodded Paint until he caught up with the Indian's pony.

"Which way are you taking the train?" I asked him.

"Tucson."

"What's a red man going to do in Tucson?" I asked.

"School." he said. "I go to be doctor. School teach white man medicine. Better than Apache. White man's medicine have great magic. Apache medicine has buffalo shit."

"I'd always heard Apache medicine men were powerful." I told him.

"Some. Others just want people to feed them."

"Oh." I said.

We rode in silence for four or five hours after that. I noticed that his pony could pick its way through the cactus and rocks without any difficulty so I wrapped the reins around the saddle horn and let Paint have his head, following the pony's lead. When it finally stopped, Skinny Horse jumped down and turned to me.

"You got coffee?"

"Yes." I said. "Make fire. I'll make coffee."

He gathered some mesquite and soon had a small fire going between three rocks. I pulled out my small pot and put a handful of coffee in it, poured in some water from my water jug and set it on the rocks.

"Hungry?" I asked him.

"Mm. Belly shrunk. Needs fill."

I dug in my supplies and pulled out two slices of jerky. I handed him one and he took it grinning. He bit off a good sized piece and started chewing.

Suddenly the entire scene seemed funny to me. Here was an Indian chewing on a piece of jerky that I had given him. His jaw working up and down like a pump handle, a grin on his face as big as Gila Bend, and me standing there watching him eat. I let out a giggle. Skinny Horse laughed. We started laughing in turn, first me, then him. I pointed at him and he pointed at me and we laughed at each other. Nothing seemed funnier to me than an Apache wanting to go to White Man School to be a doctor. I roared.

Skinny Horse roared right back, slapping his bare thighs and howling. Anyone who might have seen us standing there laughing at each other would have thought we were both loco. They would have been part right. I was loco, I was just a has been rancher with a saddlebag full of railroad money trying to return it. Skinny Horse was a young man who wanted to learn medicine to save his sick people.

CHAPTER 8

The conductor wasn't Chester Peak. He was a skinny man, in his late 40's, and nasty as an Arkansas razor backed hog. He didn't want to let Skinny Horse on the train, even though my new found Indian friend had the fare. We both argued with him, I told him flat out that as far as I knew there were no railroad regulations that said Injuns couldn't ride as long as they paid. Skinny Horse pulled a knife and held it out in one hand, his money in the other. He extended them one at a time, first the money hand, then the knife hand. I think the conductor got the meaning of that.

Then he didn't want to board our horses. He charged us ten dollars each to put them in a cattle car. We thought that was nine dollars each too much and argued about that, but in the end we paid. Hell, I've seen days I would have sold Paint for ten dollars, but now I didn't know where I'd find another horse like him, so I paid. I took the saddle off of Paint and left his blanket on his back, carried the saddle with me to a seat.

After all of that, I took the canvas bag and looked for the tellers car on the train. There wasn't one. I went back to the conductor thinking to tell him the story about my unlikely train robbery, but then I thought better of it, since he was so damned nasty, and held my tongue. I'd find a cashiers car on a train sooner or later, and then I'd turn in the cash, get a receipt and be done with it. Either that or I'd turn it in to the Sheriff in Tucson, get a receipt from him, and put an end to a train robbing career that had just started.

I walked back to the last passenger car on the train and found Skinny Horse sitting by himself looking out the window. I sat next to him and closed my eyes, used the canvas bag with the cash in it for a pillow. In minutes I was asleep. I dreamed again of Will. This time we were still kids, riding for the Confederacy. Paint was a young horse, still a little wild. In my dream, Will and an older rebel soldier helped me castrate old Paint. I'd hated to do it, but they convinced me that Paint would get wilder and wilder, especially if he caught wind of a mare in heat.

The funny part about the dream was that Skinny Horse was helping us to castrate old Paint. He had his knife in one hand and money in the other, and he was trying to do the evil deed on old Paint, but offering me money. It's crazy how dreams get all tangled with fact.

My dream drifted off to another part of the war. We had crossed a small river, Will and I, on the way to deliver a message to a General in Georgia. I looked down at the water in the river and suddenly it turned red. I looked up at Will on his horse and there was a hole in Will's chest and blood was pouring out into the river, causing the water to turn red. I yelled at him to get out of the river so I could bandage his wound. He just grinned at me and the grin was suddenly the same one he had given me as I held his head in my hands and let him sip on the canteen right before I put him on the train. I cussed myself for ever leaving him alone on that train. I should have gone with him to Tucson.

It was dark when I woke up. The train rumbled on towards Tucson, Skinny Horse still sat stoically looking out of the window. The sky was full of stars and a toenail moon looked like it was following the train westward. I couldn't get that dream out of my mind. I was hungry and thirsty and more tired than when I had fallen asleep. I got up and walked through the train to stretch my legs and to rid my mind of the dream.

I strolled up to the first car in the line behind the engine, opened the door and stood there a few seconds watching the earth pass rapidly under my feet. Then I took a couple of quick steps and was in the engine compartment. The noise wasn't as bad as I expected in there. The engineer turned away from some dials he was watching and hollered at me.

"What are you doing up here?"

"Just wanted to see how these things run," I yelled back.

He smiled at me and waved me on in. I sidled up to him so we wouldn't have to yell at each other to be heard.

He talked loudly enough for me to understand him and explained how the fire turned the water into steam, how he meted out the steam to the piston rods that pushed against the wheel cams, how the steam condensed and returned to the water boiler. It was fascinating and I thought that I might want to study to be a railroad engineer someday. But then I already had a job. Train robber. I figured I'd best return that train money first, then think about getting a job.

We talked for a while until he had to stop talking and throw more wood into the fire box. I left the engine and returned to my seat. It dawned on me that I had left the canvas bag tied to my saddle and the saddle under the seat.

I looked to see if the bag was still there and it was. I'd have to be a little more careful of that, I figured.

CHAPTER 9

Dewey Bradshaw was glad to see me. I introduced him to Skinny Horse and he didn't seem near as glad to see a redskin, but he accepted him and told him he could sleep in the loft as none of the hotels in town would rent him a room. I figured I could save a few dollars by sleeping in the loft too, so I didn't bother trying to find a hotel room.

I paid the blacksmith for the work he'd done on Paint's shoes, the hay he'd fed my horse, and the boots and britches. He figured it at about four dollars so I gave him five. He asked me if I wanted the job mucking out the stables and I turned it down. Skinny Horse accepted that position. After our business was done at the livery I helped Skinny Horse find the town doctor and was amazed when he gave the doc a small bag of gold dust to pay for his training. The old doctor looked at the gold dust and stuck it in a cabinet where he kept his medicine. He shook my hand and introduced himself. His name was Belfry. It was easy to remember him, his first name was Brad and I remember thinking that he had Brads in his Belfry.

I left them there talking as best they could, the doctor mumbling stuff about lead poisoning and infections, Skinny Horse listening intently with that sly smile on his face. I was reminded of the good laugh we'd had at each other and almost started giggling again, but walked outside and took a deep breath. I just hoped no prejudiced cowboy would gun down Skinny Horse before he learned White Man medicine.

The saloon was nearly empty when I walked in. I hadn't had a drink of whiskey in nearly two months, and that was one luxury I'd promised myself the day I ate trail dust driving my small herd to Randy's ranch. I sidled up to the bar and leaned on it, putting my right foot up on a brass rail that ran the length of the bar.

"Whiskey," I said.

The bartender was a young man, not much older than me. He put a glass on the bar and poured it half full from a bottle he took from a shelf on the wall behind the bar. I glanced at the label. Charter Oak, genuine Kentucky Bourbon whiskey. I sighed. Here I was in Tucson, Arizona drinking bourbon made back in Kentucky. I wondered if Will and I should have stayed there.

In the mirror behind the bar I saw a man sitting at a table next to the far left front corner of the room. He was tall, probably over six foot, and lean. He was dressed in a dark, pin-striped suit with a vest and a fancy shirt. His suit coat was long and open at the front. I could see his gun under his coat, it had silver handles. It was the man who had been sitting across from the seat where I'd laid Will.

I watched him for a while, judging him. He was past forty years of age, hair was black but turning gray. His face was thin. Broad shoulders, long thin arms and legs. He wore a black silk tie under a stiff white collar, little mother of pearl buttons down the front of the shirt. A real fancy dude, I thought.

The bartender had stood there with the bottle in his hand, waiting to see if I wanted to purchase a second drink. Now he spoke softly.

"That's Bill Dressler."

"Who?" I asked.

"Dressler," the bartender said. "Bill Dressler. He's supposed to be the fastest gunman in Arizona. He's killed two men right here in this saloon."

"He has?" I asked. "Gunfight?"

"Well, you could call it that," the bartender said. We were both speaking softly, sure that our voices couldn't be heard at the table where the gunslinger sat.

"What would you call it?"

"One of them never had a chance. Twas a young cowboy who called Dressler a cheat. Dressler shot him through the head with a derringer. The boy hadn't even cleared leather yet."

"Whew!" I said.

"I knew that cowboy," the bartender said. "His mother told him not to take his gun to town but he wouldn't listen."

"Is that right?"

"Yep. His name was Billy Joe. His momma was in the general store the other day. She told my wife that the last thing she said to her son was, 'Billy Joe, don't take your guns to town, son. Leave your guns at home.'"

So that was the cowboy whose boots and britches I was wearing. I didn't say anything about them, just stared at the reflection of the gambler in the bar mirror. He was also the man who might have put a slug in Will's chest. Sooner or later I'd have to ask him about that. I wanted to clear the muddy waters of the train robbery first. I thought about taking the money to the sheriff.

"Who's the sheriff in Tucson?" I asked.

"That'd be Garrett."

"Where's his office?"

"Down this road about a quarter of a mile," he told me. "You'll know it when you see the gallows next to it."

"Gallows?"

"Yep. There was a hanging last week. Sheriff hired some carpenter to build the gallows for the hanging."

"Who got hung?"

"A railroad bandit."

I almost choked on my whiskey. I coughed a few times and set the glass down hard. The bartender took that as a request for another shot of whiskey and filled the glass. I downed it.

"Yeah," the bartender was saying, "they had his trial just two weeks ago. He was sentenced to hang by the neck until dead, and that's just what happened. He didn't die when the trap was sprung, his neck didn't break, it stretched. He hung there and choked to death, wiggling his feet and dancing at the end of that rope."

I know my face was turning white. I sat the whiskey glass down easy.

"Another?"

"No, thanks. That'll do me," I said. I put fifty cents on the bar and he gave me my change.

"You're the feller that worked for Bradshaw a while aint you?"

"Yep." I said.

"You gonna work there again? I heard he still needed help."

"Nope," I said.

"What'll you do? You staying in town long?"

"I reckon I will," I said, and raised my voice enough to where I know it could be heard at the table in the front.

"I'm going to be here till I kill the son of a bitch that killed my partner."

I watched for a reaction on the face of the fancy dude at the table. He didn't make a move, no frown, no change in his face one way or the other. He just moved his nose a fraction of an inch towards me and stared at my reflection with the coldest blue eyes I'd ever seen. If looks were hooks, I'd be caught.

I didn't flinch, but stared back. Lord help me, I thought. If this is the man that killed Will he's going to have to kill me too, or I'll kill him. One way or the other.

"Iffen you're gonna kill somebody, do me a favor and kill him outdoors. I'm sick and tired of mopping up blood in here. I'm gonna start charging extra for drinks if I have to mop up the blood of one more dead gunslinger."

I figured if he raised the price a nickel a glass he'd probably make a fortune before the turn of the century.

I rolled a cigarette and lit it, scratching the match on the brass rail. I had to bend over to reach the rail with the match and that took my eye off of the mirror. When I stood up I was looking at the reflection of the fancy dude, only this time he was standing right next to me. It was if he'd just vacated one spot and reappeared at another. I've never known a man who could move that fast that quiet.

"You looking for a killer, son?" He said.

"Yep. My partner got shot under a water tank next to the tracks, two days train ride east of here. I remember seeing you sitting across from him the day I put him on the train."

If he thought I was going to back down, he had another thought coming. I wasn't in the mood to get shot, but I'm a little braver after two shots of whiskey, too.

"Well," he told me. "You can cross me off of your list."

"We'll do the crossing when the time comes," I said, looking him steady in the eye.

"Have it your way, boy," he told me. First it was son, now it was "boy". In some circles "boy" is a disrespectful name. My circle was one of them.

"If I'm a boy, why did all of those men die?" I asked him.

He looked at me long and hard. His cold blue eyes never left mine.

"Just a little friendly advice, boy." There! He said it a second time. "You might want to be a little more careful when you think you can kill men in this town. Some men just won't be killed."

He turned on his heel and with three long strides was out the door, the batwing doors swinging behind him on screechy hinges.

The bartender reached across the bar and tapped my shoulder.

It nearly scared the beejezuss out of me. I whirled fast and when I faced him my Colt was in my hand.

"Whoa!" he yelled.

"Don't touch me like that again," I told him. "This Colt might go off accidentally next time."

He backed away, his voice a whispered stutter.

"Yes sir."

I meandered out the door and down the street looking for the gallows. Next to it I would find the Sheriff's office.

CHAPTER 10

I found the Sheriff's office with no trouble. Inside, I found Garrett. His full name was Thomas Patrick Garrett.

I didn't have the railroad's money with me, but I asked the question anyway.

"What would a feller do if he had a lot of money that didn't belong to him and he wanted to get it back to the rightful owner?"

"That depends on who the owner is and who the feller is," I suppose, Pat Garret said.

I thought that was a strange answer coming from a lawman, but I waited for an explanation.

"If I had the money, I'd make sure the owner wasn't an outlaw, or someone who had got the money illegally before I gave it back."

"Well it's not my money. The owner is not one person, it's like a business."

"A bank?"

"No, at least not direct. It's the railroad."

"You're the man who held up the railroad?" he asked.

"Not exactly," I said. "I really didn't intend to hold up anyone. I was on board that train to find out who killed my partner, Will. I had a bandana over my face and my gun out. I guess the teller in the cashier's cage just took me for a bandito, and handed me the money. I really didn't know it was money until I got it home and opened the bag."

"You expect me to believe that?"

"Well now I'm telling the truth," I said. "Whether you believe me or not is up to you, I guess. I just want to turn the money over to you, get a receipt for it, and get it off of my mind and out of my hands."

"You've got the money?"

"I don't have it on me," I said, turning my hands palms up. "I know where it is."

"What's your name?" he asked me.

"Charles Merritt."

"I've heard about you," he said. I hoped it wasn't anything bad.

"You have?"

"Yes. A man was just in here a few minutes ago. He said that you might be itching for a fight. He warned me that if you started a fight with him, he would finish it."

"Dressler?"

"Yeah. You itching to fight with him?"

"Not really," I said, sighing. "I just told him that I was looking for the man that killed my pardner, Will, and when I find him, I intend to kill him."

"You shouldn't have told *HIM* that, and you definitely shouldn't have told *ME* that!"

"Why not?" I asked.

"There's law in this territory, Merritt," he said. "We do not condone killing, whatever the reason. Vigilante justice aint tolerated here. If someone killed your pardner, and you can prove it, we'll take care of the killing end."

"I've seen how the justice system works elsewhere," I told him. "In Kentucky it didn't work too well. A man kills another and the law doesn't convict him and he goes free."

"This aint Kentucky" he said. "I'm the law here. If you find anything that convinces me someone killed your pardner, you tell me. If I believe you, I'll arrest that person, depending on what evidence you have. I guarantee you that person will be tried in a court of law. If he's found guilty, he'll hang. If you kill him, you'll either hang or get a stiff sentence in a territorial prison."

"Will you take the train money and give me a receipt?" I asked.

"Bring it to me. I'll see that it gets back to where it belongs."

"That didn't answer my question, Sheriff." I said.

"What do you mean?"

"I mean, do I get a receipt signed in your hand? Something that will tell everyone concerned that I turned the money over to you."

"Don't you trust me?"

"I've only trusted two men on the face of this earth, Sheriff, since my Pa died. One is me. The other was my pardner, Will. Now that Will's dead, that leaves one. Me."

"Bring me the money, Merritt. I'll see that you get a receipt."

"I'll bring you the money," I said. "But the rest of this is between me and the man that shot Will. I'd advise you to stay out of it. This is just something I've got to do. I didn't serve in the Confederate Army to support the territorial law. Will saved my life once. I'm going to kill the man that shot Will even if it kills me, so help me."

I turned on my heel and left the sheriff's office, and when I saw his reflection in the glass on my way out he was standing there with his mouth open, looking at me.

I'd heard somewhere that Garret was the man who brought Billy the Kid down. Maybe he thought that earned him the right to tell me about vigilante justice, about how I should turn over Will's killer to him, how the territory would take care of it. He didn't know me. He may have heard of me, but he didn't know anything about me.

Like he didn't know that my Pa was considered the best shot in Kentucky with either pistol or rifle before smallpox killed him. Or that my Pa had spent hours with me before he died, teaching me to shoot straight and fast.

"Son, this is a man's world, and the man who makes his own laws will live." He told me. I remembered his words plain as day. "I'm not telling you to go against set rules. What I'm telling you is that there are times when a man has to rely on his own judgment, his own skills, and his own guns, the law isn't always your best friend, neither is the government."

I remembered clearly the day he told me to strap on his Colt. I was just 12 years of age, and barely big enough to hold the Colt. The weight of it almost made me stand lopsided with it strapped on, and the holster tied almost below my knee. I remember how he told me to pull the gun out slow, cock it with my thumb as I pulled it. He said it wasn't how fast a man cleared leather but how straight he shot that counted.

At first I couldn't hit the inside of a barn with me standing in the middle of it. Slowly but surely though, Pa taught me. He started by sitting walnuts on fence posts and having me draw, point and shoot.

"The barrel is just like your finger, boy. Just point it and pull the trigger, don't take time to aim. Your eye will tell you when its right to pull."

I practiced. Pa had an ample supply of ammunition and the Colt became like a third hand to me. After a while Pa started rolling walnuts on the ground and having me draw and shoot at them before they stopped rolling. If I didn't shoot before they stopped rolling, Pa would sigh deeply and say: "Don't worry about speed, just make sure you hit the target before it stops rolling."

I practiced some more. By the time I was thirteen Pa would stand next to me and throw walnuts out away from me. I would draw and shoot at them, the big Colt kicking my small hand up and back with each shot. After a while I learned to control the recoil by putting a little more force down on the handle and cocking my wrist a little forward. I could hit three out of ten walnuts by my thirteenth birthday. By the time I was fourteen I could hit nine out of ten. Then smallpox came and took Pa and Ma. Then the Confederacy came and Will took me.

Will was a good shot with a rifle but always found pistols intimidating.

"Give me a long rifle every time," he said. "A man with a pistol can't get close enough to me to kill me if I've got a rifle."

Of course he was right. But someone had been close enough to kill him.

I'd learned to shoot a rifle at a much earlier age. I'd often bring supper home in the form of rabbits or squirrels long before Pa started teaching me to shoot the Colt. The rifle that I shot back then was a muzzle loader 50 caliber Hawkens. I seldom missed. Pa bought lead by the pound from a coal mine boss. We melted it and poured our own balls, Pa sold them in the store.

He ran a mercantile store near the Ohio River. The town was called Caseyville. It was on a bluff overlooking the wide river. A gang of rebels had plotted to kidnap U.S. Grant's son who was staying in Caseyville, and hold him ransom. Grant got word of it and had his son moved from Caseyville to Paducah where he stayed until the end of the conflict.

My Pa was a friend of a man named Casey for whom the town was named. Casey and two other men had opened the first coal mine in Kentucky and until the war they had supplied coal for steam powered boats on the Ohio.

After the war, Will and I had tried our hand at running the store but neither of us had our hearts in it. We'd put a lot of money into buying supplies and then selling it on credit to people who couldn't afford to pay us back. It didn't take long for the store to go under. Then we went under. Under ground, working in the coal mine. Neither of us liked that back breaking work so we quit.

We tried farming for a while. That lasted shorter than the store. If it wasn't floods it was drought and every penny we put into seed was lost. All the hard work of breaking ground and planting was wasted. That's when we decided to go West.

Now I stood on the board sidewalk outside the Sheriff's office in Tucson, Arizona territory, and looked up and down the dusty dirt road. A lone rider was coming in to town from somewhere west. I couldn't see the rider but I caught sight of the cloud of dust the horse was kicking up, and could tell that the rider was in a hurry. A decade or so earlier and that rider might have been a Wells Fargo pony express rider, now the train had replaced that task. But something was making this rider move at a pace faster than it is desirable to push a horse in the heat and dry air near Tucson. I wondered what it was, so I wandered down the street to the saloon, figuring that's where the rider would rein in first.

Once there I stood with my back to the wall, pulled my dirty sombrero low over my eyes, rolled a smoke and waited.

When the rider dismounted and quickly hitched the reins of the horse to the rail in front of the saloon, I stood transfixed.

She was the prettiest woman I had seen since a nurse at the hospital in Alabama where a Confederate surgeon had worked on my leg.

"Is there a doctor in town?" She asked me.

"Yes, ma'am," I said. "If you'll allow me, I'll show you his office."

"Lead, I'll follow," she said.

I hurried away, headed down the street where I knew my friend Skinny Horse would be listening intently to the lessons of the town doctor.

CHAPTER 11

Her name was Elizabeth McAllister. She was the daughter of the most successful rancher in the territory, Sam McAllister. Sam's ranch, a sprawling 3000 acres, was west of Tucson. He had settled in the Altar Valley as a young man, married the daughter of a Tucson banker, and developed his ranch into a thriving business.

Sam had been cutting calves for branding when his saddle slipped sideways off of the horse and Sam had suffered a broken leg when the horse stepped on him. The fracture was bad enough to cause serious bleeding under the skin and Elizabeth had elected to ride for help instead of sending her father's ranch foreman, Jim Sanders. Jim had argued with her, telling her that it was a dangerous trip for a man, let alone a girl of nineteen, but Elizabeth had her father's bullheaded attitudes, and her mother's determination that anything a man could do, a woman could do better.

I learned most of that from Dewey Bradshaw.

That day she rode into town and got off of her horse in front of the saloon was the day I got sick. Oh, there wasn't anything physically wrong with me. I guess you might say I got shot. Cupid's arrow was sunk so deep in my chest a team of surgeons wouldn't have been able to cut it out.

She was both determined and physically attractive. She got my attention when she walked next to me on the way to the doctor's office.

"Can't you hurry up, cowboy?" She said.

I broke into a trot and she caught up with me.

"My father's dying and your trotting like a sick calf," she said.

I broke into a run and she caught up with me again. I turned it up a notch and when my boots were making five foot strides she was running alongside me, her moccasins kicking up dust, her strides not as long, but a whole lot faster.

We arrived at the doctor's office and she bolted ahead of me, slammed the door open and in a loud voice yelled:

"I need a doctor and I need him now. In a wagon or on horseback. We've got fifty miles to ride and no time to waste."

"Slow down just a hair," Brad Belfry demanded. "What's the matter with your daddy, Elizabeth?"

"Your Doc Belfry?" she asked. "Daddy's got a busted leg. A horse stepped on him. His leg is bad. It's bleeding under his skin and turning black. We need to ride."

Then she turned to me.

"Get me two quarts of whiskey from the saloon, bring them and my horse back here."

It wasn't a request, it was an order. I hadn't taken orders from anyone since I left the rebel army.

But I took hers. I sensed the urgency in her voice, and took off running back towards the saloon. As I ran away, I heard Doc Belfry yelling at Skinny Horse to hitch his horse to a buckboard behind the office.

By the time I got back with the whiskey and Elizabeth's horse, the buckboard was loaded with Doc's wooden medicine chest and his horse was hitched to it.

"Get your horse and follow us," the doctor told Skinny Horse. "This will be a good lesson for you. Now hurry!"

Elizabeth hitched her tired horse to the back of the buckboard and climbed up beside Brad Belfry on the seat.

"Heeyi!" Doc yelled and slapped the horse with a long whip.

The horse reared a little, settled down and took off at a fast trot.

Skinny Horse looked at me, grinned, and said, "You go too?"

"I hadn't thought about it," I said. "But hell yes. I'll go."

We ran to the livery stable and found our horses, saddled and mounted them and rode out together, following the cloud of dust made by the buckboard. I figured it couldn't hurt anything to make acquaintance with the beautiful girl's daddy since I fully intended to marry her.

CHAPTER 12

It was a long day's ride to Sam McAllister's ranch and we hadn't left Tucson till after noon. By the time it got dark Doc Belfry stopped the buckboard.

"If I try to drive this thing in the dark we'll never make it," he said.

"I'll go on then," she said. "I'll have Dad ready when you get there. You may have to amputate his leg."

"You'll do no such thing, young lady!" Doc said. "There's renegade Apaches out there that would love to get their hands on a prize like you."

"I'll take that cowboy who rides the paint horse with me," she said. "We'll make it."

I knew she was talking about me and I had mixed emotions. I wanted to ride with her, but I knew Doc was right. The two of us wouldn't be much of a match against eight or ten renegade Apaches. Only one thing we had in our favor was the dark. Apaches don't like fighting in the dark.

I had already dismounted and started to take the saddle off of Paint when Elizabeth McAllister said that she and I would go on.

"Don't unsaddle that horse, cowboy," Doc said. "If she's determined to ride on, you'd best ride with her. We'll leave at first light."

I pushed the saddle back over Paint's back and cinched it back up.

"You got water?" I asked her.

"Two canteens full," she said. "Lets ride."

She took off at a fast gallop and I had to spur Paint to make him catch up. He was tired and his tail was danged near dragging his tracks out but her horse was more tired so we caught up quickly.

"We'd best trot," I yelled. "I just lost a packhorse that stepped in a gopher hole!"

She slowed her horse to a trot. It was a large black stallion, sleek looking and powerful. It amazed me that a girl her size could handle a horse like that.

She wore denim pants under a split leather skirt, moccasins that a squaw might like and a long sleeved man's shirt. A bandana was tied around her hair that hung in a long ponytail down her back.

Slim and trim, she fitted me to a tee. I was totally immersed in her beauty.

"You trot if you want to," she yelled back at me. "I've ridden this trail since I was knee high to a jackrabbit, and I can ride as good as anyone."

With that she kneed the stallion and it took off again at a fast pace. It was all Paint could do to catch up and I was eating her dust most of the way. I didn't mind though. I rode directly behind the stallion, figuring if it fell I could swerve Paint enough not to step in the same holes, trip over the horse or step on the girl.

On and on we rode, her leading me following. After a bone jarring hour and a half, she slowed to a trot, then a walk and finally stopped the stallion with a gentle "Whoa".

"We'll rest and let our horses blow," she told me. "There's water here."

"Where?" I asked, looking all around.

"Right over that dune," she pointed in the direction we had been riding. "Just a trickle, but enough to let the horses drink. I wouldn't advise you drinking out of it, there may be a dead critter upstream."

I walked Paint towards the water steam and she caught up on the stallion. We both dismounted and let the horses drink while we took drinks from one of the canteens. She drank first, and I could swear I tasted the sweetness of her lips when she passed the canteen to me.

"How old are you?" She asked me, suddenly.

"Twenty five," I said. "At least I think I'm twenty five, I don't keep track of months or years too much."

"You ought to know how old your are!" She said.

"Well I'm twenty five, then." I said. She had more or less ruffled my feathers by berating me. I momentarily wondered if she'd make a good wife after all, but threw those thoughts aside immediately. She was the best looking woman I'd seen west of the Mississippi, and I wasn't going to let a few words distract me on my intent to marry her.

"How old are you?" I asked.

"I'll be twenty in a month." She said. "How old do I look?"

"Twenty in a month," I said, smiling.

She laughed. It was a full hearted, genuine laugh. I looked at her and smiled broadly. It was nice to know that I made her laugh. She sidled up to her horse and opened a saddlebag, almost having to stand on tiptoe to reach it. She extracted two strips of fried meat and gave me one, along with a piece of bread. It was the most delicious bread I had eaten since before my Ma died, and I told her so.

"Well I'm glad you like it," she said. "Now let's get back on the trail. My father's leg won't get any better by itself. He needs me there."

"Yes ma'am." I said.

CHAPTER 13

We arrived at the ranch at sun up and Elizabeth sat about immediately ordering me around. Build a fire. Boil some water. Wake up the bunk house. Tell the foreman she wanted to see him. I was tired, hungry and in a grumpy mood and all I wanted to do was curl up in a ball somewhere and sleep for two days. But I wanted to show her that I could take it. Not the orders, but the physical duress she had undergone. If she could do it, I could.

The foreman was a tall, strongly built man named Jim. He had a droopy moustache and wore a ten gallon hat that seemed too small for his big head. It was securely tied on by a chin strap with a sliding wooden bead on it to keep the hat from blowing in the wind. If I thought I was a grump, he was two grumps rolled into one.

In the bunk house he cussed me out for waking him. The rest of the hands just yawned and stretched and scratched and grumbled. Jim cussed and fussed and farted. When the other hands waved their blankets towards him to clear the foul odor out of the bunkhouse, he blamed me, and cut loose with another round of cussing.

"Who the hell do you think you are rolling in here waking us up?" he demanded.

"I'm just following orders," I said.

"Who's orders? I'm the damned foreman here, I give the orders!"

"Elizabeth." I said.

That seemed to shut him up. He mumbled a lot but got up and got dressed.

"She wants to see you in the house," I told him.

"Oh she does, hey?" he yelled. "I work for her daddy. If he wants me, he knows where I'm at."

"Her daddy may lose his leg today," I said. "The doc from Tucson is on his way here, and from what I've been told he may have to amputate that leg."

"I know that, you greenhorn," he yelled, throwing a boot at me. I dodged it and picked it up and handed it back to him.

"Where'd you come from?" he asked.

"Just happened to be standing in front of the saloon when Elizabeth rode in yesterday," I said. "She commandeered my services to find the doctor for her, then insisted on riding back out here in the dark. The doc said it was too dangerous with word of renegade Apaches around here. She recruited me to ride with her."

"Well stick around, greenhorn," he said. "With the boss down I'll need an extra hand. I'm sure he'll agree to signing you on, that is if you want to ride for me."

"I'm no greenhorn," I said in my own defense. "I have a small spread northeast of Tucson. I've worked it for the past four years. Nothing grand but it's a start. I just sold my stock last week so I can finish some important business, then I might move on to California."

"What business is that?" he asked.

"Finding a killer," I said. "Someone put a slug in my partner. I intend to find out who the skunk bag was that done it. When I do, I'll finish my business, then I'll decide what I want to do."

"You best be leaving law matters to the law," he said. "Sign with us. If you find your killer, I'll help you take him in."

"I won't need to take him anywhere," I said. "The only place he'll be going is to hell."

He looked at me long and hard.

"Have it your way, cowboy," he said. At least he didn't call me greenhorn after that.

He got dressed and I walked back to the ranch house with him. Elizabeth was waiting in the kitchen. She was standing at the window looking out towards the east for a cloud of dust that would signify the buggy carrying the doc and my Indian friend.

"Jim, I'm going to need all the help you can give me to save Dad's life," she said. A determined look spread across her beautiful features and she glanced at me, then nodded in my direction.

"This man is good with horses and you can use him. Get him a spot in the bunkhouse and an extra horse. He's nearly ran that paint of his into the ground to get back out here with me. Make sure Blaze is fed and rubbed down, get the men to work, then come back here. I'll need you to help hold Dad down if the doc decides to take his leg."

"Yes, ma'am," Jim said, holding his ten gallon hat at waist level with his two big gnarled hands.

She turned to me.

"If you want a job, you're hired."

I didn't hesitate. All I wanted at that particular time was to stay near to her. I could find Will's killer anytime, but to find another woman like Elizabeth would take a lifetime.

"Thank you," I said.

"The pay is twenty a month. Food is good and you'll be given another horse. You're free on Sundays, and your birthday. Jim's the foreman, you'll take orders from him. Payday is on the first of the month."

"Yes ma'am," I said. "Pardon me, but do you want me to stay here and help with the doctoring this morning?"

"Jim will stay." She said. "The other hands will show you where to pick out a horse. It'll be up to you to break it if it needs breaking."

"Yes ma'am." It was all I could think of to say.

"There's the wagon!" she said, excitement in her voice.

I glanced out the window and saw the cloud of dust rising in the west.

Something seemed wrong to me. There was a small dust cloud all right but behind it I could see a larger cloud of dust.

"We'd best ride out to meet it," I said. "It looks like they've got trouble!"

Elizabeth looked out the window again. Realization of what was happening struck her as it had me.

"Indians!" she said.

Jim looked.

"Come on, cowboy!" he said and ran out the door. I ran after him and he let out a yell.

"Saddle up!" He yelled. "Injuns!"

CHAPTER 14

Ranch hands ran towards the corral, drug saddles down from the top rail and started cutting their ponies out of the crowd. I had left Paint tied to a rail near the kitchen porch, still saddled, with enough slack in his reins to reach a water trough.

Within minutes ten horses were saddled and men were checking their rifles. I mounted Paint and pulled his reins loose from the rail.

"Heeyiii!" Jim yelled and we took off eastward, riding hard, toward the dust clouds.

Paint was tired and stiff from the long night's ride, but still was able to keep up with Jim's horse as he led the ranch hands. The wind was blowing from east to west, the cloud of dust from the wagon carrying Doc and Skinny Horse was blowing towards us, and behind that another cloud of dust being kicked up by thirty or so Indian ponies. We could hear the screaming from the Apache band over the pounding of our own horses hooves. I'd heard similar sounds, coming from squadrons of mounted soldiers raiding rebel camps.

The narrow trail I had traversed in the opposite direction was rough in places and I could see Doc bouncing on the buckboard seat and whipping his horse while Skinny Horse was hanging on for dear life. I wondered how he felt being pursued by his own kin, no doubt, and running away. No doubt he would be tortured if he was caught, first for being a traitor to his people and second for being a coward. Indians hate cowards.

I could see Skinny Horse's pony tethered to the buckboard and as the group of ranch hands parted to let the buckboard through, Skinny Horse rose from his seat and took two quick steps to the back, unhitched his horse and swung out and dropped astride it. He gripped the horses neck with his knees and turned it in a circle to join the bunch of us who were now firing our rifles at the oncoming Indians. He rode up next to me and made a motion with his hand and forefinger, pointing towards the Indians, then towards my colt. I drew the colt and kneed Paint close enough to hand it to him. He drew the hammer back and as we neared the renegades, he spurted ahead of the rest of us, rode directly into the group and fired a shot into the chest of one of the Indians.

They wouldn't torture *this* Indian for being a coward, I thought. I saw him block a thrust from a long pointed spear, fire a shot into that Apache, and jerk the spear out of his dead hands.

I was busy firing my Henry at oncoming renegades and lost track of what Skinny Horse was doing, but in the dust of the fight I was worried that one of the ranch hands I was riding with would shoot my friend. Then I realized that Skinny Horse was not wearing his Indian garb. His hair was tied at the back of his head and hung down inside his shirt. He looked just like one of us except for his complexion.

We were outnumbered three to one but the fierceness of our attack, and coming out of the dust cloud that had been blowing towards us, caught the raiding party by surprise and what was left of them turned tail and ran. We gave chase for a quarter of a mile or so, then reined up. I looked ahead and Skinny Horse was still in hot pursuit of the renegades. I gave a long, loud whistle, forcing the air between my teeth as hard as I could. I saw him turn his horse and he came racing back to where I sat on Paint.

When he was thirty yards away, one of the cowboys riding near me raised his rifle and pointed it directly at Skinny Horse.

I switched ends of my Henry, grabbing the hot barrel with my left hand and swung it in a quarter circle and caught the cowboy on the shoulder, causing him to fire a shot wildly at the sky.

"Damn you!" he yelled at me, "What'd you do that fer?"

"He's a friend!" I yelled back.

Then I yelled to the rest of the group who were reining up their horses nearby.

"Hold your fire!"

Skinny Horse rode up alongside Paint and handed me my Colt.

"Shoot good!" he said, smiling.

"You did good, my friend," I told him.

"This man is a friend of mine," I yelled at the group. "He's not a renegade, he's Doc's student of medicine."

"He's a damned Injun!" The man I had hit with my rifle bellowed out.

"He's a human being," I yelled back at him. "If you've got a problem with that, take it up with God."

The man looked at me with eyes blazing.

"Apaches aint human," he said. "They's heathen and savage. They attacked our wagon train on our way out here, killed several people, including women and children. Then they burned the wagons. I was lucky to get away."

"Let's suppose you had stayed wherever you started from," I said. "Then let's suppose a bunch of white men moved in and tried to take your land, burn your crops, shoot your herd. What would you have done?"

"Why I'd of joined forces with others and drove them away!" He said.

"That's just what the Apaches were doing," I said.

"Injun lover!" He snarled at me. "Get down off that horse and face me like a man!"

I swung my leg over the saddle and dropped to the ground. He dismounted and handed his reins to another man. The whole crowd was watching us. I looped Paint's reins over his head and dropped them. He wouldn't move more than twenty feet.

Jim nudged his horse closer to the two of us but said nothing. A circle of horses formed around us, some men were still mounted, others stood holding their horses reins. It got very quiet suddenly.

I was dead tired from an all night ride, fixing fires, carrying water to boil, and the ride out to chase the renegades away from the buckboard. I didn't want to fight anyone, but I felt like I had to take a stand.

"You two men have at it," Jim said, breaking the silence. "The rest of you, keep out of it. I'll fire the first man that interferes."

I was watching the man approach me, he was walking on the balls of his feet like I'd seen a prize fighter walk back in Kentucky. My daddy had always told me to watch the center of my opponents chest. He said that any motion would be seen there first.

I saw a slight twitch of the man's shirt on his right. I brought my left arm up fast, bent at the elbow, fist straight up in the air and swung it hard out and away from me to my left, catching his blow and knocking it away. I hit him hard right on the nose with my right fist, and quickly backed away. Blood spurted from his nose. He yelled obscenities at me and charged, both fists swinging wildly. I sidestepped his charge and kicked him hard in the gut with my right foot. He doubled over, gasping for breath.

I stepped behind him quickly, booted him in the butt and watched as he fell face forward in the dirt.

I turned my back on him and walked towards Paint who had wandered a few steps away.

"Charlie!" I heard Skinny Horse yell.

I spun around and saw the man still on the ground, his right hand held his pistol and it was coming up toward me.

My hand flashed to the Colt, drawing it up, right thumb had the hammer cocked by the time the barrel cleared leather, forefinger on the trigger. I didn't have time to aim. I pointed, like my Daddy had taught me. The colt roared and blood spurted from the man's hand. He screamed in pain and flung his hand backward, gun twirling away.

"Next time you draw on me, I'll kill you," I said.

Men stared at me. No one spoke.

I holstered the Colt and took my neckerchief off and tied it tightly around the man's wrist. He squirmed and tried to get away.

"Get away from me!" he hissed through clenched teeth.

I ignored him and tied the knot tighter around his wound. The bullet had creased his thumb, but hadn't hit bone. He'd be fine in a week or so.

"Let's ride," Jim said, reining his horse back towards the ranch house. Soon the entire band of hands were galloping away, leaving me there with the wounded man and Skinny Horse.

"See that he gets back OK," I told my Indian friend, then I mounted and rode after the ranch hands.

CHAPTER 15

"Well you'll have to do the work of two men now," Jim told me.

"Why's that?" I asked.

"You shot one of my men. He was a good worker, he can't work with one hand. You'll be hard put to take his place."

"I'll not try to take his place," I said. "He was going to shoot me, I got off a shot in self defense. Whatever he's got, he deserves."

"We'll see what the boss says," Jim said and walked away.

I could see that I was going to have a tough time if I wanted to stay on at this ranch.

"Where is my student?" Doc yelled at me when he saw me.

"He's coming, Doc," I said. "He'll be bringing in another patient. A man with a flesh wound on his right thumb."

"Snake bite?" he asked.

"No, Colt bite," I said. "He tried to shoot me. I shot first."

"Well I'm going to need some help," he said and walked towards the house.

I followed him, ignoring my previous orders from Elizabeth to pick a horse out of the corral.

When we got to the kitchen, Elizabeth greeted Doc and motioned towards another part of the house.

"He's in there," she said, and walked towards another room. She opened a door and held it open after walking through, the doctor followed her. I started in but she shut the door in my face.

"Stay here," she said. "We'll call if we need you."

I stayed.

It seemed like just a few minutes when the door opened again and Elizabeth told me to fetch the whiskey. I went back to Doc's buckboard and found it and brought it to the bedroom and knocked softly on the door.

"Come in," she said.

I went in and handed Doc the two bottles of whiskey. He sat one on a table and opened the other and poured two fingers into a glass.

"Drink this," he ordered and handed it to a man who was laying on the bed. That must be Elizabeth's father, I thought. The man took the glass and drank it down, non-stop. Doc poured another one.

"Drink this if you can," he said.

"You pour, I'll drink," the man said in a weak voice.

"Not too much at a time, now." Elizabeth said.

"Let him drink it," Doc said. "The quicker he passes out the better off he'll be."

"I know a little about medicine," she said. "If he drinks too much whiskey at one time it could kill him just as surely as gangrene."

So Doc is going to amputate, I told myself. I didn't want to stay and watch but it looked like I was drafted.

It was just at that point when Jim knocked on the door and Elizabeth opened it.

"I've got the redskin here," he said.

"Send him in," Doc said, loudly.

"Thank the Lord," I said under my breath.

Skinny Horse went into the room and stood at Doc's right shoulder.

"Wash your hands good," Doc told him and he turned to a basin of hot water and dipped his hands, picked up a bar of soap and commenced to lather his hands.

"Gimme another one, Doc," the man on the bed commanded.

Doc poured another glass of whiskey and handed it to him. He drank it in three sips and laid back down, the glass slipping from his hands. Elizabeth took it and set it on the table.

"Dad," she said. "Are you still conscious?"

"Mmmm," he muttered.

She bent over his face and looked closely at him.

"He's been awake all night with the pain," she said. "He'll be asleep in minutes."

"White man's medicine is whiskey?" Skinny Horse asked.

"Just to put him to sleep," Doc said. "Fetch my box of tools, Merritt," he told me.

I left at a fast pace and returned to the buckboard. There was a wooden box that was made of cedar, I hefted it and heard rattling inside. I picked it up and carried it on my shoulder back to the bedroom.

Doc unlatched it and started laying tools out on the bed. Each piece was shiny like it had just been polished. The box was lined with a white silky cloth and I could smell some kind of disinfectant emanating from it.

"Can I go now, Doc?" I asked.

"You can go or stay," he said. "I won't need your help, but if you want to learn how to amputate a man's leg, this will be a good lesson."

"I've seen it done before, Doc," I said. "The hospital I was in during the war cut more legs from men than I want to remember."

"Yes," he said. "I did a lot of surgery then. Which side were you on?"

"The wrong one," I said.

"There wasn't a right one," he told me.

That brought a new round of respect for Doc from me. I took a deep breath and let it out slow to keep the tears out of my eyes, turned and walked out of the house, and across the yard to the bunkhouse. I didn't care what Jim or anyone else said, I needed to sleep a while, and that's what I did.

CHAPTER 16

The horse I picked out of a herd of wild horses was a mare. She didn't particularly like me, although I fell in love with her right off. She was roan colored with a little white diamond shape right between her eyes. When my rope settled around her neck like a string of pearls, she stood there looking at Paint like he was a long lost beau or something, then she kicked up her heels and loped away until she reached the end of the rope. She jerked her head twice, then bucked and kicked several times.

I had taught Paint to hold his ground and I dismounted, worked hand over hand down the taught rope until I was ten feet away from her. I took off my hat and held it out to her. When she moved from my right to my left, I moved the hat from left to right. If she moved back, I moved the hat back. What I was trying to teach her was that if she moved in the direction I wanted her to, the rope would slacken and wouldn't bite into her neck. She caught on real fast, and within minutes if I moved the hat to my left she moved to my left.

I finally held the hat right straight out in front of me and kept it still. She sidled back and forth a few times, then stopped directly in front of me and watched the hat. It didn't move, so she didn't move. I kept the hat extended and walked slowly to her. When I was close enough I made a motion with my hand and the hat, just a slight movement, a brush motion, away from me very slightly. She backed up two steps and stopped.

Then I brought the hat close to my chest and held it there. She took two steps forward. It seemed like she was going to be easier than I thought to break, but I guess I misjudged her. I motioned with the hat towards my body and turned my back on her and walked away with the hat held close to my chest. The rope was slack around her neck and I expected that she would walk behind me to keep the slack in the rope. I was wrong. She took off in the opposite direction, jerking my arms around, since I was holding the rope in my hands. I spun like a top on my boot heels. She had her tail towards me and kicked her hind legs high in the air. I moved towards her quickly to give her some rope slack.

She kicked again, then turned to face me. I walked closer, giving her more slack.

We danced back and forth for several minutes until I was able to win her confidence by showing her that I would give her room to move. Then after a while I was stroking the little white diamond between her eyes with my gloved hand, and letting her sniff my other hand. She whinnied a little and snorted a little, but seemed to settle down and accept my presence near her head. I extended my hand further up, scratched between her ears, and then slid my hand down to her jowl and patted her there gently. She jerked her head back once, then thrust it forward. I patted her again.

I didn't realize that I had an audience. Men were watching me work the horse. It wasn't but a few more minutes when I was leading her towards the wooden corral fence. When I got her there I made a quick hackamore with the rope and slipped it on her nose and head. She sidled away from the fence when I looped the rope over it, but didn't jerk. A saddle and blanket were on the top rail of the fence a few feet away, and I slipped the blanket off and carried it to her, holding it out in front of me as I had previously held my hat. It was easy to put the blanket on her back. I left it there and returned the few feet and went through the same motions, carrying the saddle.

I eased the saddle up and let it down gently on her back. Her head snapped around and she got a funny look in her eyes but stood still. I put my left hand on her neck while I reached under her belly and looped the cinch strap through the buckle. It didn't bother her a bit when I cinched the saddle up tight. I took the rope loop free of the fence and put my left foot in the stirrup and swung up and as gently as I could, settled my weight in the saddle.

That's when she decided she'd had enough.

She kicked the board rail at about the top level, crow hopped a few times, went straight up and did a complete body twist and came down on all fours, then bucked again. I hung on, knowing that at any moment she would take off running. She jumped up again, spread her legs almost straight out and when she landed, she was on her back legs, front legs high in the air and kicking. Then she dropped to all fours again and took off.

A cowboy opened the corral gate and she ran out and headed towards the open range. She was nearly as fast as Paint, running smooth and with a rhythm that I could adjust to easily. I leaned forward in the saddle, gave her slack on the hackamore and let her run. I thought she'd never stop.

I looked ahead and saw a cloud of dust coming towards us about two miles away. Indians, I thought, another raiding party! But I was wrong. The mare ran straight towards the oncoming riders and when she was twenty yards away the party split and she stopped. She bucked a few times and then stood still as the horses from the group of riders settled around us.

One of the riders was Garrett.

"New horse?" he yelled.

"Yep, my first time on her," I turned the roan's head and urged her back towards the ranch. When she was a few yards from the group of riders, I raised both feet in the stirrups and kicked her in the sides, at the same time I leaned forward and slapped the rope on the side of her neck. She took off again, headed back towards the corral. The riders behind us urged their horses to a trot and by the time they reached the corral I had dismounted and removed the saddle and blanket. I was rubbing the mare's nose when Garret spoke to me again.

"Charles Merritt, you're under arrest."

I looked at him, wondering if I'd heard right. He sat on his horse holding a piece of paper. The other riders, six of them, were behind him and evenly divided on either side of him. He dismounted and stood leaning on the corral gate.

"Arrest?" I said. "What for, I've done nothing to be arrested for."

"Train robbery," he said. "You confessed to me that you robbed the train. I got a complaint from the railroad, and here's a warrant for your arrest, signed by the Marshall of the territory."

"I didn't rob the danged train," I said. "I told you how it happened, and I said I'd give the money back. Things have happened that prevented me from doing that."

"You told me that, I agree," he said. "That doesn't mean you are innocent. I'm here to take you in. You'll get a trial."

I heard the door to the kitchen slam shut and Elizabeth walked out.

"What's going on here, Sheriff?" she demanded.

"This man is under arrest for train robbery," he told her.

"Train robbery? You must be mistaken, Sheriff, this man helped save my father's life. If he hadn't ridden back here with me and fought renegade Indians to protect Doc Belfry, my father might have died. As it is, we've just finished amputating his leg and he may recover."

"I'm sorry about your daddy, Elizabeth, but this man confessed to robbing the train," Garrett said.

"There must be a mistake," she said.

"I did confess to having the money," I said. "I told you I had no intention of robbing a train. The cashier on the train handed me a bag and I didn't realize it had money in it till much later."

"You were armed," Garret said. "You told me you had your pistol in your hand and a mask over your face."

"That was to keep people from recognizing me if I killed the conductor." I said, then realized I was getting deeper into hot water.

"You killed the conductor?" Elizabeth asked, disbelief in her voice.

"No, I didn't kill anyone," I said. "I might have if he'd been the one who shot Will."

"Who is Will?" she asked.

"You can talk to him in jail," Garrett said. "Now get your horse, Merritt, you're going with me."

I glanced around and saw Paint standing in the middle of the corral, saddled and rested. I thought of running, but there were six men with Garrett and I didn't think I could get out of the corral unless Paint could jump the top rail. That didn't seem like a good idea to me, so I gave in.

"I'll go with you, Garrett," I said. "You know I didn't rob that train. I'll get the money and give it back. I wish I'd done that earlier, now."

"Give me your gun," Garrett said.

"I can't do that. I'll leave it with Elizabeth, if she'll take it, but I'll not give up this gun. It's been with me too long."

"Will you keep his gun, Elizabeth?" Garrett asked.

"I will," she said. "He'll be back to join our crew. I don't think he's guilty of anything, let alone train robbing."

CHAPTER 17

After the long ride back to Tucson, Garrett locked me in a cell.

I didn't get a chance to go get the money. I had hidden it in a very secure spot. In the loft of the barn at the livery there was a spot where boards were nailed to the corner post. There was a space between the boards just big enough to stuff the canvas bag with the money. Money from sale of my cattle was in it along with the money from the train.

I was starting to get a little scared. I remembered the story about the train robber who was hung on the new scaffold outside of my cell window. The rope hadn't broken his neck when he fell through the trap door and he had strangled to death, dancing like a puppet on the end of the rope. Grisly death, I thought. I hadn't killed anyone either, but now I wasn't sure if Elizabeth knew that or not, and my fear for my life was growing by the hour.

There was nothing I could do to help myself. The only person I knew in town besides Doc Belfry who was still at the ranch nursing Elizabeth's father back to health, was Bradshaw, the blacksmith. I asked the sheriff if he would tell Bradshaw to come see me.

When he came to visit he brought me a piece of fried chicken and a piece of pie. I thanked him for it, and listened as he berated me for boarding the train to question the conductor.

"I told you to let it be, boy," he said. "Now you are in jail. You wouldn't listen to me." He ranted on and on for a few minutes until I stopped him.

"That's past." I said. "I'm in jail and I need to get out. Now are you going to help me, or not?"

"I'll do what I can," he said.

"If I tell you where to find the money they say I stole will you fetch it here and give it to the sheriff?"

"You know I'll do my best," he told me. "If I didn't like you, son, I wouldn't be here now."

I was grateful for that, but more grateful for the pledge to bring the money sack. I told him where to find it.

"Make sure that Garrett is here when you bring it in," I said. "And make him sign a receipt for it to show that I willingly returned it."

"OK."

"One other thing," I said. "I've got money in that sack that belongs to me from selling my cattle. There's a hundred and sixty five dollars that is mine."

"I'll hold it for you," he said. "You can trust me, Charlie."

"Thank you, Mr. Bradshaw," I said. "You are a good man and a good friend."

I saw a tear in the corner of his eye as he turned and walked away from the bars that held me prisoner. He was my only chance now to get out of this cell and ride back to the ranch where I wanted to be. I had impressed Elizabeth, I thought, and with the help of the Good Lord, I intended to marry that girl.

Two days went by and I hadn't heard from Bradshaw. No one had brought me any news of any kind.

I was really starting to get anxious now. I asked Garrett if he'd seen Bradshaw and he said he hadn't, but then he'd been out of town, riding on another posse to catch a horse thief.

The afternoon of the third day a man I knew walked into the Sheriff's office, Garrett wasn't in, and the man took a look around, saw me in the cell and spoke to me.

"Find your killer?" he asked.

I had been half asleep, the afternoon sun was shining through a high window in my cell and falling on the wooden bunk. An old wool blanket was my only mattress and I was napping when I heard the voice. I thought I was dreaming, until I opened my eyes and saw him standing at the bars, looking in.

It was Dressler.

"What did you say?"

"I asked if you'd found your killer yet," he said. "If you found him and killed him, maybe that's why you're locked up."

"Not that it's any of your business," I said, "but no. I haven't found my killer. I'm in here for train robbery."

"Robbed the train, did you?"

"No, I did not," I said, vehemently. "I'll be out soon. I'm waiting for a friend to prove my innocence."

"How's your friend going to do that?" He asked.

"Let's just say that isn't your concern." I said.

"Well, have it your way," he said, and walked out of the building.

I wished I hadn't been so curt. Someone to talk to was better than no-one to talk to, and Dressler was an interesting character, even though he might be the man I was seeking, Will's killer.

I started to call after him as he left, but something in me wouldn't let me do it. I'm not a proud man, just that I have some feelings about certain people, I can usually tell if I'm going to like a person or not, and I didn't like Dressler. He was bad news to me, even if he wasn't the man who shot Will. He was a gambler, and had killed other men. That made him dangerous and a little on the shady side. After I thought that, I considered what I would be if I ever did find out who killed Will, and gunned him down. Then I'd be a killer. Can't be helped, I thought. A man has to do what a man has to do.

I was deep in thought about the philosophical essence of life, and why my life had been cut out the way I'd lived it until now. I didn't hear the door open, and had my eyes closed. I heard a soft sound, like the shuffling of a shoe on a floor, and my eyes opened.

Elizabeth stood at the barred door, looking at me.

"Elizabeth," I said.

"Hello, Charles," she said. "I've brought you some lunch. I hope they've been treating you good here."

"Can't complain," I said, "Except I don't belong in here. I didn't rob any train, and I will prove it when my friend Bradshaw returns with the money they say I stole."

"Bradshaw won't be coming back, Will," she said softly.

"What? Why not?"

"He was found in the livery two days ago," she said. "A cowboy found him. He'd been shot. They took him to Doc Belfry, but Doc couldn't save him. Before he died,

Mr. Bradshaw told Doc to tell you that he was sorry. Someone held him up and took a bag of money he was bringing to you."

"My money?" That was all I could say. Then I thought of Elizabeth and the reason I had met her, the ride out to her ranch and her father laying near death in a bedroom off of her kitchen.

"How's your father?" I asked.

"He's going to live," she said. "Thank you for helping me get back to him, and thank you for fighting off that bunch of wild Indians. Doc Belfry said he wouldn't have made it had you not led the charge against them."

"Jim led that charge," I said. "I was just part of the riders that rode out there."

"That's not the way Doc tells it," she said. "He told me you rode ahead of the bunch and that you shot one of my men because he was going to shoot Skinny Horse."

"Well, I'm guilty of that," I said.

"Your Indian friend was a great help to Doc Belfry and myself when we took Dad's leg," she said. "But it was you who helped the most."

She looked at me like I was Ulysses S. Grant or somebody. I blushed.

"I didn't do anything special," I said.

"Well, here's your lunch, Charles," she said softly. I walked to the bars and she handed me a cloth wrapped package through the door bars. It was heavy and I thought at first she was giving me my gun.

"Thank you," I said, and smiled at her. "If I ever get out of here, I'd like to come see you again."

"You're welcome at our ranch. Dad wants to meet you, and Jim says you'll make a fine hand."

"What about you, Elizabeth?" I said. "Do you want to see me again?"

She looked quickly away, then back at me.

"Yes," she said, then turned rapidly and walked away from me.

"Elizabeth," I said, hurriedly.

She didn't stop. She walked right on out the door. I felt my heart skip a few beats. She had told me she wanted to see me again. I was certain that she had some feelings for me that I know I felt for her.

I took the package and sat on my bunk and unwrapped the cloth. Inside was another package, on top of it was a ham sandwich, made with a thick piece of smoked ham and a slice of the homemade bread we'd had the night we rode to her ranch.

I sat the sandwich aside and opened the cloth on the second package. It contained a double roll of coins, wrapped in a thin material. The material came off easily and I counted the coins. There were 50 of them. Each one was gold and had the $20 U.S. mint stamped on it. A thousand dollars.

That was a start, but I didn't think it would be enough to buy my way out of jail. I wondered where Elizabeth had got such a sum of money. More than that, I wondered why she had brought it to me. She'd told me that my money, along with the $3000 in paper money that I'd asked Bradshaw to fetch, was gone. Now I had to get out of jail. More than one mystery had reared its ugly head.

Someone had killed Will and now someone had killed Bradshaw and stolen more than $3000.

CHAPTER 18

Two more people came to see me while I was in jail. Doc Belfry and Skinny Horse. Doc was amiable, thanked me for helping him get through the renegade redskins and brought me up to date on Sam McAllister. He had lost the leg. The operation performed by Doc was just in time to stop the gangrene from spreading. Skinny horse had found some tools in the shed behind the bunkhouse and using a piece of wood that had fallen from the corral, he had fashioned a pair of crutches. He shot a jackrabbit, skinned it and used its brains to cure the hide. He cut strips of the hide and sewed soft portions to the crutches. Sam was able to get out of bed on his own and walk on crutches to the kitchen. It would be a long time before he'd be able to ride, but Doc said that Sam was tough and wouldn't be one to sit around.

Jim had vowed to hire me back if I wanted my job. He'd forgot about me shooting one of his hired hands and wished me well.

I wanted desperately to get out of the jail, and told Doc. He talked to the sheriff and the two of them made some kind of agreement that if I paid something called "bail" in legal terms, I could sign a document agreeing to appear before the territorial judge on a given date. If I failed to show up on that date, the "bail" money would be forfeited. Not being a lawyer, I wasn't sure how that worked but agreed readily to pay the bail. I hadn't mentioned the thousand dollars that Elizabeth brought to me, but when Doc offered to pay my bail I told him I could pay it. Bail was a hundred dollars.

Garrett drew up some papers for me to sign and I signed them readily. He said that I could leave, but reminded me that the territorial judge would be in Tucson in a month and I'd have to appear before him. The judge might order me placed in custody again until trial.

But I was free!

I thanked Doc profusely for helping me and slapped Skinny Horse on the back. We pointed at each other and laughed like a couple of school boys for a few minutes, then shook hands. One of Bradshaw's oldest boys was running the livery and had taken care of Paint. I paid him, using one of the $20 gold pieces and saddled Paint. I carefully wrapped the remaining gold pieces in the cloth Elizabeth had brought them in, and put them in my saddle bags. I certainly didn't want anything to happen to that stash.

Elizabeth was heavy on my mind. My heart ached to see her and to thank her for bringing me the gold. I didn't know where she had got it, and it didn't matter, but I intended to give the remaining portion back to her with a promise to repay the rest. It had been a week since she'd been in town and that week seemed like ten years. A deep longing ache crept up inside me, a feeling of emptiness, like there was something missing in me. I knew that it was her whispered "Yes" when I had asked her if she wanted to see me again. I hoped I wasn't making to big of a deal out of that one little word, but my heart wouldn't let me think otherwise.

I rode Paint to the saloon and tied him to the rail. Inside, I said hello to the young bartender, bought a whiskey and took it near the front window so I could watch my saddlebags. I sat down at a table next to five men who were playing cards. One of them was Dressler. He glanced at me but didn't speak. The other four didn't pay any attention to me.

When the hand was finished, Dressler looked at me.

"Well, well. If it isn't the Train Robbing Kid."

The other four men looked at me then. One of them smiled and then turned his head and spit into a brass spittoon.

"Bring some of the railroad's money over here," he said. "I'll be the one called the man who took the Train Robbing Kid's money."

They all laughed.

I sat silent.

"Care to join us?" Dressler asked. "Fred, here, might have been jesting, but I'm in earnest. You do play poker, don't you, boy?"

I had played. During quiet times, sitting around campfires during the war, I'd learned to play. We didn't have much money then and the stakes were never high. Most of the time we played for matches. On occasion we would play for pennies. I'd learned the game.

"I play," I said.

"Join us," Dressler said. "Can't cost you much. Twenty dollars will get you in the game."

I thought about it for a minute, not saying anything. I watched them play instead. The man called Fred was dealing. He sat facing me, another man, fat and short, sat with his back to me. Dressler was on his left. Two tall cowboys sat on the other side of the table, one facing Fred, the other half turned so that he was looking at the fat man but watching me.

I watched the hand progress as the cards were dealt. I could see the fat man's cards but not any other players, except the cards that were on the table. The fat man was dealt a pair of sixes and had a six up. He didn't raise until the last card was dealt, Dressler called and Fred called.

The fat man turned his hand up and announced, "Three sixes."

The other men folded their hands. The fat man raked in the chips.

"This could be your pot," he said, looking at me. "All you have to do is play. You can't win anything if you aint in."

The thought of winning enough money to pay Garrett the railroad's money was tempting me. I had a fairly good knowledge of how to play poker, but the way my luck was running lately, I hesitated.

"Of course if you're scared to wager, you can't win a cent," Fred said.

That raked across a nerve and I stood up slowly. I was thinking that if I went to my saddle bags for money, everyone in town would soon know I had some money. I'd have to make sure no one held me up, shot me, or bushwhacked me like they did Bradshaw.

"Be right back," I said, and walked out to Paint. I opened the saddle bag and was careful to only get a $20 piece. If I lost that, I'd quit. I felt a little guilty about gambling with Elizabeth's money, but if I won, I'd be able to pay her back.

Back inside I flipped the coin on the table and said, "I'm in."

I took a seat between Fred and the fat man. Since Fred had just dealt he passed the cards to me.

"New blood can't deal," one of the cowboy's said, and the other agreed.

"You deal, John," Dressler told the fat man.

John took the cards from me and shuffled them. I watched as his stubby fingers manipulated the cards expertly. He offered the deck to me for a cut and I cut them.

I didn't win the first hand, nor the next. By the time I did win a hand I got just enough out of it to where I was back almost even. Then my luck changed. I won three hands in a row. Now I was five or six dollars ahead in the game.

One thing I had learned about playing poker is that you never want to drink and play. Alcohol makes your mind fuzzy, you lose track of what cards have been folded, you make risky bets, you throw your money away and when you start to lose, you throw good money after bad. Being sober, the right way to play is to bet a winning streak. When the cards are falling your way, ride it for all it's worth. Luck is fickle and can change instantly, so while you've got it, play it.

Two hours later I was a hundred dollars ahead.

By the time it got dark and the young bartender came around and lit oil lamps so we could see to play, I was two hundred dollars ahead. Everyone at the table was grumbling about my good fortune except Dressler. He didn't say anything, one way or the other. He played his cards and when I wasn't winning, he won. Fred dropped out of the game. John was getting drunk and the two cowboys were hanging on. One of them was nearly broke, the other had won enough to barely hang in the game.

Another gambler took Fred's place, bought in with twenty dollars and won the first pot he played. I took the next pot and Dressler the next. On the next hand, the new gambler was dealt a pair of aces showing and bet them heavily. I stayed in the hand with two hearts in my hand and two on the table. On the sixth card I caught the Ace of hearts. Now I knew that the new gambler didn't have all four aces, three's the most he could have. I worried about him having a full house the way he was betting, but stayed in, not raising, just calling.

After the seventh card fell I was pretty sure that I had the winning hand. I'd seen the other ace fall to one of the cowboys. The flush was well hidden, three on the table and two in my hand. Dressler was staying with a possible straight showing, and the new gambler had drawn a pair of fours to go with his pair of aces. He raised twenty dollars after the opening bet. I called and Dressler folded.

"Two pair, read 'em and weep." he said.

"That don't beat my flush," I said and laid down the hearts I held in my hand.

He stared at me for a few seconds.

"I ought to blow you in two for that," he said.

I froze.

"Hold on, Blacky," Dressler said. "You're not talking rational. The boy just beat you, that's all. Nothing personal."

"He called my hand even though I could have had a full house!"

"Yes, he did." Dressler said. "And I folded my straight because I read his hand. He had three hearts on the table after six cards. I could have beat your two pair, but not his flush."

"I still think he's trying to make me look bad," Blacky said.

"I'm not trying to make you look any way at all," I told him. "You play your cards and I'll play mine. If I win, that's my luck. If I lose, that's still on me."

"You don't know who you're talking to," he said through clenched teeth.

I wondered if he was going to draw on me. My gun was being held for me by Elizabeth. I didn't even have a holster strapped around my waist.

"The boy's not armed," Dressler said. "Calm down, Blacky."

"Well, it's a damned good thing," Blacky said. "Next time I see you here in town, be packing," He looked hard at me when he said that.

"I've got no call to carry a gun just cause you say so," I said. "You just told me that I don't know who I'm talking to. That's true, I suppose. But I do know this about you. You are a poor loser. If you ever draw on me, you'll still be a poor loser."

Blacky stood up suddenly, his chair falling over behind him. As his right hand flashed toward his gun I heard Dressler yell.

"Hold it!"

Blacky's hand froze halfway to his holster. I glanced at Dressler and he had his long pistol on top of the table, pointed at Blacky's chest.

"I told you he wasn't armed, Blacky," Dressler said coldly. "Is that how you got your reputation, shooting unarmed men?"

Blacky stood there staring at Dressler's gun. His right hand started to tremble a bit. Dressler waved the long pistol at him and told him to sit down.

"Keep out of this, Dressler," Blacky said.

"Or what?" Dressler asked. "You won't draw on me. I'd kill you in a heartbeat. You and I haven't been the best of friends ever, and I won't hesitate to shoot your belt buckle off if you ever draw that gun on me."

"You've got the drop on me," Blacky said. "Can you outdraw me in a fair fight?"

"I just did," Dressler told him. "And there aint nothing fair about drawing on a man that aint wearing a gun."

Blacky stood looking down at Dressler for a few seconds then turned and walked away. He went to the bar and ordered a whisky and downed it.

Then he walked to the front door, turned and looked at me.

"I'll take care of you the next time we meet," he said.

I kept quiet.

After he had left the bar, I asked Dressler about him.

"He's got a reputation as a gunslinger," Dressler said. "One that he is proud of, but probably doesn't deserve. He'll get himself killed one of these days, and that'll be the end of Blacky. His real name is Jack Christian, but I've always known him as Black Jack Christian, or just Blacky."

"Why did you pull your gun when he started to draw on me?" I asked.

"I hate a fight that aint fair," he said. "I play honest cards, and I've been in some honest gun fights. I always play fair and I expect everyone else to play fair."

"So you wouldn't shoot a man who was dying?"

"You talking about Will?"

"Yes," I said. "You know what I'm talking about."

"I told you before, Charlie. You're barking up the wrong tree."

It was my turn to deal and I dropped it. I was starting to believe that Dressler had nothing to do with Will's death. But if it wasn't him, who was it?

I dealt the cards.

CHAPTER 19

Early the next morning I was on my way to the McAllister ranch. I had won nearly five hundred dollars in the card game. Enough to pay back the money Elizabeth had brought me, and then some. After deducting the thousand dollars she had brought I had four hundred and eighty dollars left. Not a bad nights work.

I figured that I could get to the ranch about sundown if I kept a steady pace and didn't get attacked by Indians. Paint was fresh as a daisy and wanted to lope so I let him. It was a beautiful morning. The sun cast a long shadow ahead of me as I followed the railroad tracks west. When I came to the point where I had to veer off to the right and head slightly north, the sun had risen to a point almost directly above me. I stopped for a while and had a bite to eat, fixed a pot of coffee over a mesquite fire and let Paint chew on bits and pieces of sage grass.

I sat hunkered over the fire, drinking my coffee, thinking about the series of events that had led me to this point.

The one thing that I didn't understand, other than who shot Will, was who had held up Bradshaw and stole the train's money, along with mine. Someone must have known Bradshaw was going to bail me out by returning the money. It had to be someone who knew he was going to go fetch the money and bring it to the sheriff's office. Could it have been the sheriff himself? I turned that over in my mind a few minutes. It didn't make sense. Pat Garret was a well known and well liked sheriff. He was given credit for killing Billy the Kid, although some think that he didn't give Billy a fair fight. I liked Pat Garret, enough to trust him. I didn't think it could have been him that shot Dewey Bradshaw and stole my money. Or the train's money.

As I was thinking all of this I heard the westbound train coming. It was a mile or two behind me, but the distinct sound whispered to me from the ground. Then I heard the chatter of the wheels on the rails and by looking back to my left I could see the curl of gray smoke that the engine spit out as it chugged west to Tucson.

Someday I'd like to take Elizabeth on that train and go all the way to California, I thought. We'd find a quiet little valley out there somewhere and start a farm. We'd have a couple of boys and a girl or two to help around the place. My imagination was working overtime. I could feel the warm glow in my chest when I thought of Elizabeth. I remembered how she had looked standing there holding the lunch with the gold coins. She was beautiful and smelled of scented soap. Her hair was the color of clover honey, and shined like the sun at high noon.

I'd had a girl friend when I went to school before my folks died and I rode away to join the rebel forces. Her name was Judy and she was as cute as a butterfly on a rose. She had a sparkling laugh and never seemed afraid of anything to do with romance. She had kissed me the first kiss I ever got from anyone other than my mother. Her breath always smelled like cinnamon buns and her lips were as soft as clover. I thought that I loved her more than anything else in the world but when it came time to go I left without another thought of her, just got up and left, not knowing what fortune would fall me, and not thinking about ever returning to kiss those clover lips again.

After the war, when Will and I returned to Kentucky to try to run the store, I saw her once. She'd married and was happy, and I was pleased that she was happy. I had never thought about her kisses until now.

Now I was wondering what it would be like to kiss Elizabeth. Would her breath smell as sweet as cinnamon buns? Would she laugh softly like the night I told her she was "twenty next month" when she asked how old I thought she was? Would her lips be softer than clover?

When things got straightened out with the railroad's money, the jail time, and the man who killed Will, I intended to ask Elizabeth to marry me. There wasn't any other way to stop this longing, throbbing feeling that I woke up with every morning since the day I'd met her.

I shook my head and poured what was left of my coffee into the fire and got up. I raked sand over the fire, turned and looked at Paint.

"Come on, old Paint, let's get where we aint!" I said, laughing out loud at myself. I swung up on Paint's back and headed towards McAllister's ranch where I hoped I'd see Elizabeth standing on the kitchen porch waiting for me.

CHAPTER 20

It was sundown when I reached McAllister's ranch. Elizabeth was not standing on the porch waiting for me. No one was waiting for me. I headed Paint for the corral and took the saddle off and slung it up on the top rail. I rubbed him down good, fed him and made sure he could get to water.

In the bunkhouse a few cowboys had already hit the sack. I guessed that supper was over and berated myself for not riding a little faster. I was tired, hungry, and a little bit melancholy because I had really wanted to at least see Elizabeth's face when I rode in, but reality was that I am just like any other cowpoke, so I found my bunk and took off my boots and trousers and rolled in. In minutes I was fast asleep.

The sound of the triangle rapping out a staccato ring woke me up. I could smell bacon frying and got up hurriedly, pulled on my trousers and boots and walked out to the privy for a quick relief, then headed for the chow line. Jim saw me coming and came to greet me, his big hand stuck out to shake mine.

"Welcome back, cowboy," he smiled. "I didn't think I'd see you again till your hangin'."

"Sorry to disappoint you, Jim," I said. "But I'm not ready to get hung yet, I'm innocent until proven guilty."

"That you are, cowboy!" He said, slapping me on the back. "Anyway, let's get some grub and I'll show you what I want you to do today. You'll be riding fences with Younger."

We got plates and utensils from a stack on a wooden table, made our way through the line at the chuck wagon, and returned to the table to eat. I was nearly starved and the bacon and scrambled eggs and flapjacks went down fast. I was wondering if I was allowed to go get a second helping when Jim said,

"There comes Younger. I'll introduce you."

A tall, thin cowboy walked towards the table carrying his plate of food. He was not gaunt, but thin. He was taller than me but his clothes hung on his thin frame, making him look thinner than he actually was.

"Younger, this here is Charles Merritt. He'll be riding fences with you for the next couple of days. Merritt, Younger is a good hand, he'll show you what I expect."

"Howdy," Younger said.

"Hello." I said in return. "You been with this outfit long?"

"Yep, I guess you could say that," he said. He was a pleasant looking man, easy smile, dark eyes. His hair was coal black and hung down past his shirt collar. His sideburns were long but other than that he was clean shaven. I felt the three day growth on my own chin and wished I'd taken the time to shave.

"You the feller that they say robbed the train?"

"That would be me," I said. "Although I didn't rob anybody. I was trying to get some information from the conductor, and like a fool, I was wearing a bandana over my face, and had my gun out. The danged cashier just threw a bag of money at me. I was in a hurry to get off the train since my horse was tied to a swing rail. I didn't even think about the bag having money in it."

"Why'nt you give the money back then?"

"I was going to. I had it hid in a safe place and a friend went and got it for me. Unfortunately he was gunned down and the money was stolen. I'll catch the snake that shot my friend and clear my name, if it's the last thing I do."

"Well if it was me I'd be doing that instead of riding fence line," he said.

"I'll be riding back to Tucson soon enough," I said. "That's where I'll start looking for the killer. Whoever shot my friend probably knows about who shot my partner. I've got two killers to look for."

"Your partner?"

"Yes. I was working a small spread with my partner, Will. He got sick with a appendix problem and I took him to the train and put him on it. Somebody shot him for the twenty dollars I put in his boot to pay a doctor fee."

"I heard about that," he said, glancing away.

"Who'd you hear that from?" I asked, curious.

"Elizabeth told me," he said.

That surprised me.

"Elizabeth?" I said.

"Yes. She told me about that. Too bad about your partner, Merritt. Also about your friend. I wish you luck in finding the killers."

He got up and walked away, carrying his plate back to the chuck wagon where I saw him get more eggs and bacon. I grabbed my plate and ran after him.

"Hold on," I said. "What else did Elizabeth tell you?"

"Not much more about you," he said, helping himself to more flapjacks.

I got more eggs and bacon and helped myself too.

"She was talking about me but that's all she said?"

"Well, we were just talking about her daddy. She mentioned you were a big help in getting the Doc and that Indian out here. She went on to tell me about how you were arrested and put in jail."

"That's all?"

"Yeah. I got a little upset with her, talking about you. I guess it showed and she quit talking about you then."

"You got upset? Why would you get upset?"

"We was on a little picnic out to a private place, I didn't think it was right for her to talk about another man while she was with me."

I didn't say anything. Elizabeth had been on a picnic with Younger to a private place? That news made the eggs and flapjacks settle like horseshoes in the pit of my stomach. It didn't dawn on me until now that there might be someone else in Elizabeth's life besides me. I felt lower than a lizard's tail. Gloom settled in on me like dust. I finished my breakfast, although my hunger had turned to a sour taste in my mouth.

When we went to the corral to get our horses is when I got a little bit sourer towards Younger. He threw a rope around the roan filly that I had broke and started to put his saddle on her. Whoa, I thought. It's one thing to take a man's girl, but entirely different subject when the man takes your horse.

"Whoa," I said, grabbing his arm as he started to swing the saddle up.

He let the saddle drop to the ground and turned to face me.

"What's wrong with you?"

"That's my horse." I said.

"Says who? I brought this horse down out of the hills along with twenty more wild horses. Jim said we could take our pick and I picked this one."

"She'd already been picked," I said. "Jim told me to pick a horse the day Garret came and arrested me. I picked this roan and broke her to saddle. Even rode her out a mile or so."

"Well, that's just your tough luck," he said. "I'd already had nibs on this roan. I've been eyeing her since the day I brought them in."

"If you wanted her, you should have broke her," I said.

"I would have, but I got sent back out the next day. When I returned you had already broke her. That don't make her yours, though."

"I say it does."

"What you say don't count," he said coldly. "Now get your hand off of my arm and let me saddle *my* horse."

"You aint saddling that horse," I told him. "You want a horse, you break it!"

That's when he swung at me.

I blocked the punch and hit him hard in the gut. Before I could dance away from him, he wrapped his long thin arms around me and lunged, pushing me down hard on the ground. Horses shied away from us, the roan backed away a half a dozen quick steps and stopped, eyes wide.

We rolled in the dust and horse manure of the corral, grasping arms, hands, hair, whatever holds we could find. I punched him a few times in the face and he returned the flurry. My left eye felt cut and was blurring. I could see blood trickling from his nose.

I wrangled my legs around his long thin ones and locked my ankles together. That took away the leverage he had with his legs, but mine were tied up holding his. I used the strength in my arms to roll until I was on top, then swung hard at his chin with a short right punch. It connected and his head snapped back on the ground. He swung his legs up, lifting me off of him, and as quick as a whip he grabbed me around the neck and punched me hard twice in the side of my head. His bony fists felt like clubs hitting me.

Suddenly a shot sounded close by.

Both of us stopped struggling and looked up.

Jim stood there, his pistol in his hand pointed at the sun.

"Get up!" he told us.

We got up.

"I don't know what started this, and I don't care," he said. "But if I see you two fighting again, you'll both be fired! I aint got time to be busting up fights."

"He's trying to saddle that roan," I complained. "I broke that horse, you saw me do it."

"I drove that horse in here from the hills," Younger said.

"I don't give a damn about that horse," Jim said. "Both of you find another horse. Leave that roan alone. Now get at it, or ride off this ranch and don't come back."

I felt like taking that advice, but thought better of it and saddled Paint.

"Am I still riding with this horse thief?" I asked, pointing at Younger.

"You calling me a horse thief?" He said and started at me again.

I sidestepped his charge and danced away.

"STOP IT!" Jim roared. "Younger, get on a horse. You ride with Fats today, Merritt, you'll stay here and work with me."

Younger found his own horse and started to saddle it.

"I'll settle with you later," he told me.

I kept quiet. It wouldn't do any good to keep talking. I had my idea about whose roan that was, and he had his, and we were probably half right. One of us would have to give in somehow, but the thought of him picnicking with Elizabeth was reason enough to draw the line about the roan.

He finished saddling his horse and swung up on it.

I watched as he walked the horse to the gate and another cowboy opened it for him. I looked around. There were eight or nine ranch hands who had seen the fight. The same ranch hands had seen the skirmish with the man who didn't like Skinny Horse the night we fought the renegades. I had a sinking feeling in my stomach again. I might be losing Elizabeth and at the same time these cowboys who might have been good friends probably thought I was a trouble maker now.

I saddled Paint and swung up on his back. I nudged him towards the corral gate and a cowboy opened it.

"Where you going?" Jim asked. "I said you stay here and work with me today."

"Sorry, Jim," I said. "I don't like the company here, yourself excluded. I can't work with a horse thief and that's what Younger is. Get rid of him and I'll come back."

"Now hold on just a dag blamed minute…"

I didn't hear the rest of what he was saying. I can't find out who killed Will by riding fence line or following a ranch foreman around, and falling in love with a girl could wait. I had a man to kill first. As I rode past the kitchen porch, Elizabeth stepped out.

"Charles," she said. "Where are you going?"

"Back to Tucson," I said. I reined Paint to a stop and got off, took my hat off and got her gold coins from my saddle bags.

"Thank you," I said, handing her the package. "I'd like my gun back, please."

She went inside and returned with my pistol and holster.

"Charles, why aren't you staying? I thought you liked it here."

Her eyes looked at me with a pleading look.

I strapped on the holster, checked the gun to make sure it was loaded and stuck it in the holster.

"Jim will tell you," I said, and swung back up on Paint.

I headed Paint west and rode slowly away.

"Charles?" I heard her say, but didn't turn. She would just have to wait.

CHAPTER 21

I pushed Paint pretty hard on the ride back. I had two reasons for hurrying. First, I wanted to put as much distance as I could between me and Elizabeth for fear that I'd do something stupid and turn around and go back. Second, I didn't want to spend the night alone in the desert. A man can get killed by Indians trying to ride alone. I wanted the security of being someplace where if I was going to die there'd be someone see me and maybe put me in the ground proper.

I hadn't thought much of dying since the war. Once Will and I had fought our way out of a tight spot. After having been chased by a Yankee scouting party all night, we'd holed up in a barn on an abandoned farm. Near daybreak the Yankees surrounded the barn and someone hollered at us to surrender.

"If we surrender they may kill us anyway," Will said. "I don't feel like going out without a fight. How about you?"

"We probably can't get away," I said. "Our horses are in here but they'd gun us down if we tried to run."

For the first time since I'd left home and joined the Rebels, I felt fear. "I don't want to die," I told Will. "I've got too much life ahead of me, I hope."

"Nobody ever wants to die," Will said. "But from the moment we are born we start to die. When we take that first breath of life, we have just so many more breaths to take until the last one. I believe that if we've lived a clean life and followed the teachings of the Bible, that last breath is not so bad after all."

"Will, I've always felt that the Bible is the best book to learn by, but I'm not anxious to go to heaven this morning."

"Then lets fight," he said. "If we surrender, we're dead anyway."

"How do you suppose to get *OUT* of here?" I asked.

"I've got an idea," he said. "It's dangerous but it might work."

"Let's hear it," I said.

"Help me stack this hay in front of the barn door," he said and started moving a stack of hay to the opening.

I grabbed another pitch fork and helped. It took a few minutes but when the stack was as high as the door, Will stopped me.

"That's high enough, I hope," he said.

He told me to mount up.

"When I holler, ride through that hay like you was scared of the devil," he said, "Take a hold of the other end of this rope and when we go through the door, separate and spread out."

When we were on our horses, he lit a match and threw it at the bottom of the hay pile.

The flames on the hay stack grew fast. Will edged his horse to the barn door and kicked out. The barn door swung wide.

"Now!" he yelled.

We rode. As soon as we were out, we separated and spread apart, each of us holding the rope.

Coming through the flames like the boys from the fiery furnace, we surprised the four Yankees who were waiting outside.

They got off a couple of wild shots as we rode past them. The rope caught them near their shoulders and dragged them off of their feet.

"Ride hard!" Will yelled and let go of the rope.

I urged my horse hard and caught up with Will, took a quick glance back and saw the Yankees struggling to get to their feet. I knew by the time they caught their horses we'd be gone.

Fear will get a man killed. Will used a level head and got us out safe.

I thought about that night as I neared Tucson. The sun had gone down and it was starting to get cool. I'd pushed Paint hard all day, but another hour and I'd be there, throwing down a whiskey in the saloon. My bones ached and I was hungry, but then after thinking of the times Will and I had rode together in the war, I felt more sad than anything.

I'd lost Will. Then I'd met Elizabeth and had a chance to ride with a real ranch crew, doing work that I'd grown to love, and now I'd lost that. The future didn't look too bright. I had no idea how to go about finding the man that shot Will or the one who'd gunned down Bradshaw. I had enough money to last me for a couple of months if I was careful with it, so time was on my side.

Gut empty and growling, heart empty and aching, I trotted Paint into town, found the streets void of people and only a few lamps showing here and there. Of course the saloon was open. I rode past the saloon to the livery and took Paint's saddle off, fed him and watered him. Then I made sure I had my money in my trousers and walked slowly to the saloon.

I'd expected to see a card game going on but was disappointed. A man sat at a table near the front of the room with his head on his arms, his arms on the table, and a nearly empty bottle in front of him.

Another man stood at the bar talking to the young bartender.

They both looked around as I pushed the batwing doors and walked in, making the screeching sound as the doors swung back and forth.

"Mr. Merritt," the bartender said.

"Yep," I said. "Whiskey."

He poured me a shot and sat the bottle down near me.

"One will be enough," I said and he took the bottle away.

I drank the whiskey down and rubbed my face. I needed a bath and might need the Doc to take a look at the gash in my eyebrow that Younger had made with his bony fist. But more than anything, I needed food.

"What've you got to eat in here?" I asked.

"A little stew," the bartender said. "I can heat it up for you if you'd like."

"I'll eat it cold," I said. "Any bread?

"Crackers."

"That'll do."

He brought me a bowl of stew that was thick with grease and a handful of soda crackers. I wolfed down the food without tasting it.

"Where's everybody?" I asked, glancing around.

"Aint you heard?" The bartender asked.

"Heard what?"

"Indians. They attacked here the day before yesterday and burned part of the town. Every able bodied man is out with Garrett trying to track them down."

"Indians?"

"Yep. They hit here at daybreak and burned houses and the school on the east side of town, killed four men and a boy."

"I'll be damned," I muttered. I wondered how long the townsfolk would be out on a posse chasing the renegades. Too danged weary to think about joining them, I told myself.

I paid for my food and drink and left, meandered to the hotel where I'd had my first bath in Tucson. The clerk who had eyed me naked in the bathtub was at the main desk and she spoke to me as I came in.

"Why aint you chasin' Indians?"

"Just heard about it," I said. "Can I get a bath?"

"Bath's are a dime now," she said. "Water is scarce. We used a lot of water trying to fight the fires the Indians started."

"I'll pay the dime," I said.

"You know where the tub is," she said. "I'll fetch more water directly."

I ambled in to the room where they kept the tub and was surprised to find that the water in it looked almost clean. I pulled my boots off and stripped the filthy clothes off of my body and got in the tub. The water was cold but I didn't care. I found a small piece of soap on the floor and lathered myself from head to toe, trying to get the smell of horse manure, dry sweat and campfire smoke off of myself. I scrubbed my hair good, dunked my head under the water, and came up blowing water and soap away from my face.

The bath woman was standing there holding a kettle of hot water. She looked at me long and then poured the water into the tub. It was hot enough that I had to ease my body backwards to keep it from burning my belly. She poured slowly, watching my body. I could see something in her eyes that seemed like she was enjoying the view.

"You married?" She asked.

"No ma'am." I said. "At least not yet. Maybe won't be if things don't change."

"What things?"

"Well, I'm planning on marrying someone, but I'm not sure that someone is planning on marrying me."

"Why don't you just forget about that someone," she said, smiling.

She was pleasant looking enough, and the way she was talking made it plain that she would be available for my satisfaction if I pursued it.

"I can't forget her," I said. "Since the day I laid eyes on her, she's all I can think about, mostly."

She finished pouring the water and turned on her heels and walked away.

"Too bad," she said.

I sat in the tub for a long time wondering if I should just accept the bath woman and forget about Elizabeth, or forget both and concentrate on finding Will's killer. By the time the water got cold in the tub, I hadn't really decided on which path to take. My mind told me to find Will's killer. My body told me to accept the bath woman's offer. My heart told me that Elizabeth was the most important thing in my life.

I got out of the tub and rubbed down with a rough cloth that served as a towel. I pulled on clean trousers, took my money from the dirty ones and gathered up the clothes I'd had on. As I walked past the hotel desk I asked the bath woman for a room, paid for it, and signed the register. I left the dirty clothes with her and money to have them washed. Then I climbed the stairs to the second floor, unlocked my room and went to bed, too tired to think about anything, almost. Anything except Elizabeth.

CHAPTER 22

I slept like a baby. It was nearly 9 by the grandfather clock in the lobby when I went down for breakfast. The hotel had already served breakfast that morning at seven and I was out of luck unless I could find someplace else that would serve it. I wandered down the street, noticing as I walked that a lot of the businesses were open, there was a bustle of people walking the streets and it seemed like things were back to normal. I reached the Sheriff's office and stepped in.

"Howdy, Sheriff," I said.

"Hello Merritt," he said, amiably. "What brings you back to town so soon?"

"I was going to ask you the same thing, Sheriff." I said. "Did you catch any of the Injuns that raided and burned?"

"We caught up with two that had been shot during the attack," he said. "They were barely alive then, but they're dead now. We hung them."

"Without a trial, Sheriff?"

"Injuns don't get a trial after they raid and murder townsfolk," he said.

"Were they Apache?"

"Yes. They were Chiricahua Apache," part of Geronimo's clan."

"I hope the townspeople don't try to take vengeance on Skinny Horse."

"They tried," he said.

My blood ran suddenly cold. I hoped that the sheriff was telling me that any attempt to extract vengeance against my friend was unsuccessful.

"What happened?"

"A bunch of drunks went to Doc's office and demanded that he send his student out. Doc fired a blast from an old twelve gauge over their heads and they scattered. That was the end of that."

"Good for Doc," I said, sighing. "All Skinny Horse wants is to learn the white man's medicine. He knows that the days of the redskin is numbered. As long as they resist the westward movement of whites, the white men will continue to make war on them."

"I don't get involved in redskin politics," Garrett said. "I've got a job to do and I do it, red, white or black. If a man breaks the law in Tucson, he has to answer to me."

"Well, good day, Sheriff," I said, tipping my hat.

"Stay out of trouble," he warned me.

I found a place that served meals all day long and ordered a big breakfast, eggs and bacon, biscuits, and coffee, and pancakes as big as a plate. I ate until I was stuffed, drank several cups of good hot coffee and felt like a million dollars when I paid my quarter and walked out.

I made my way slowly back towards the saloon, ambling along the wooden sidewalk, looking in store windows and taking my time. In one shop I found a dress that I thought Elizabeth would like. It was peach colored with a high bodice and neckline, sleeves that would come down just past her elbows, and a pair of white lace gloves. The dress length was just about right, I guessed, for her height, and I told the shop owner I wanted it. He looked at me like I was crazy and boxed it up for me.

"That'll be eight dollars," he said.

I paid him and asked him to hold the package for me in his store until I came for it. He wrapped it in brown paper, tying it real pretty with a silky ribbon that he charged me a quarter for. I paid the quarter and gave him my name. Elizabeth would love it, if I ever got enough nerve to give it to her.

"In case I never come back for this, after a year, I'd like it given to Elizabeth McAllister," I told him. He looked at me over the top of his spectacles, wrote the name on a piece of paper and stuck it under the ribbon before putting the box under the counter. I saw him write, "after one year give this to Elizabeth McAllister".

I headed on down the sidewalk, pleased at myself for buying something for Elizabeth, but wondering if I'd live long enough to see her wear it.

In the saloon a card game was going in the same corner where I had played a few days prior. Some of the players were the same, including Blacky. I watched the game from a nearby table, sipping on a whiskey. Blacky gave me several dirty looks, but I glared right back at him and after a while he gave up and paid attention to his cards.

Blacky lost steadily. His luck ran from worse to terrible and he lost some good hands to better hands. Those are the kind of losses that will kill you in a poker game, I know, I've been there. That's when you have a straight and someone has a flush, or you have a flush and someone has a full house or a higher flush.

After about two hours of steadily losing, Blacky announced that he'd be back, to keep his seat warm for him.

"That seat is as cold as a well diggers ass, Blacky." Fred said.

"Take his chair," John told me, motioning to the empty chair.

"No," I said, "I'd rather watch him lose as me."

Everybody laughed.

Blacky returned carrying a white, heavy cloth bag. My eyes were glued to it. It looked like the bag the train's money had been in.

He sat the bag down on the table and opened it.

I could hardly believe my eyes. *It was the bag I'd hidden in the livery loft that contained my money as well as the train's money.*

My first impulse was to ask Blacky about the bag, but a split second of reason flashed through my mind and I got up, stretched like I was tired of watching, and walked through the batwing doors slowly, listening to them screech on their hinges.

Once outside, however, I hurried away from the saloon then broke into a dead run all the way to the sheriff's office. I didn't know if I'd find him there, it was late in the evening. Usually, however, Garrett hung around in his office until near midnight every night. I was in luck. He was there.

I ran in, out of breath, and Garrett looked up at me.

"Whoa there," he said. "What's the rush? Somebody shootin' at ya?"

"No." I said, and took a deep breath. "Blacky just walked into the saloon with the bag that had the train money in it!"

"What?"

"The train's money!" I said. "The bag that Bradshaw was bringing to me when he was gunned down!"

Garrett got to his feet, took his holster and gun from a hook and strapped it on.

"Show me," he said. We left his office, me at a dead run.

"Slow down," he hollered. " He'll still be there when we get there."

I slowed to a fast walk but Garrett was still falling behind.

"Dang it, Sheriff," I said. "You told me to tell you if I found Bradshaw's killer, and now you're walking like a lame duck."

"You don't know he killed Bradshaw," Garrett said. "There's probably more than one money bag with the railroad's name on it."

"It's the one all right," I said.

"We'll see," he said.

When we walked slowly into the saloon, people looked up and saw Garrett.

"Evenin' Sheriff," Dressler said. Others around the table nodded to Garrett.

"I won't interrupt your game long," Garrett said. "I just need to ask Blacky some questions."

"What about?" Blacky said.

He had a sizeable stack of cash in front of him and a fresh supply of poker chips.

"Did you bring that cash in here in a bag? A railroad bag?"

The eyes that were on Blacky suddenly looked at me. All of the men here knew my story about the train robbery. It didn't take them long to realize that I had fetched the sheriff.

"I don't know what you're talkin' 'bout, Sheriff," Blacky said.

"You don't mind standing up then, Blacky?"

Blacky pushed his chair back slowly away from the table and stood up. The bag fell from his lap to the floor, but Garrett saw it drop.

"That bag right there," he said.

John was setting next to Blacky and raked the bag to his chair with his boot, picked it up and dropped it on the table. Blacky's face turned a pale shade of gray.

Garrett picked up the bag and hefted it in his hand. There was still money in it. He opened the top and poured the bills out on the table.

"That's a lot of money from playing poker, Blacky," Garrett said slowly.

"I've carried that cash from El Paso," Blacky said.

"What's that dark stain on the bag, Sheriff?" I asked.

Garrett held the bag closer to his face and looked at it. Near the bottom of the bag was a dark brown stain. I figured it was Bradshaw's blood.

"Well, looks like a bloodstain to me," he said. "You'd better come with me, Blacky."

Blacky's hands started to tremble and he got a strange look in his eye like he might have been thinking of drawing on Garrett. Before he could decide, Garret spoke.

"Unbuckle your gun belt and let it drop to the floor, Blacky," he said.

Blacky did as he was told and the room fell suddenly silent. Nothing but the chunk of the heavy holster and gun hitting the floor resounded in the room.

"You're under arrest for suspicion of murder, Blacky," Garrett said.

"I aint killed no-one," Blacky muttered.

"We'll let a jury decide that," Garrett said. "I'll get this bag over to Doc Belfry and let him tell me whether that is blood on it. If it turns out that stain is blood, I'd bet it is from Dewey Bradshaw."

A murmur swept through the room. The poker players were glancing at each other, then at me. They realized that if Blacky was the one who killed Bradshaw, then he may have been the one that killed Will. I had sworn to gun down Will's killer.

CHAPTER 23

While the sheriff was locking Blacky in a cell, I walked over to Doc Belfry's office to see if he was still up. A light was on so I knocked on his door.

He appeared at the door still fully dressed, his spectacles setting on the bridge of his nose and a book in his hand. I couldn't see the title but it had a picture of a human body embossed on its leather cover.

"Charles," he said.

"Hello Doc," I said.

"What brings you over this time of night? Oh my, what happened to your eye?"

I had forgot about the gash over my eye.

"Just a little fist fight," I said. "It's nothing."

"Well let me take a look at it," he said, and swung the door open. I went in and turned to face him.

"It ain't my eye that brings me here, Doc," I said. "The sheriff just arrested a man for killing Bradshaw. He had a bag that looks like the one that Bradshaw was carrying, with the money from the train robbery. Not that I robbed the train, but the one with the railroad's money in it, as well as my money."

"Yes, go on," he said, holding a lantern closer to my face. "Sit down there, Charles," he said, motioning to a chair. I sat.

He went to a desk and set his book down, turned and walked to a basin.

"Tell me about the bag, Charles," he said as he washed his hands.

"Well I noticed it when he went and got it from his horse to get money to play cards," I said, trying to remember what was running through my mind at the time.

"I thought it looked like the bag, so I went and fetched the sheriff."

"Good for you," he said. "Let me take a look at that eye."

He bent over me and held the lantern a little closer, then hung it on a hook a few inches away from my face.

"This will hurt a little," he said and pulled part of the skin from the gash down while he swabbed it with a purple looking ointment on the edge of a clean cloth. It burned like hell.

"The bag had a dark stain on it," I said. "I believe it was Bradshaw's blood. Without that stain the bag could have came from anywhere. Can you tell if it is blood?"

"Where's the bag now?" he asked.

"Garrett has it over at the jail," I said. "He's going to bring it to you, but that may not be until tomorrow. I wanted to ask you tonight and I'm glad you're still up."

"Sit still now," he said. "I'm going to put some stitches in that eye cut."

I tried to sit as still as I could but it hurt when he ran the needle through the flesh above and below the gash and pulled the flesh together.

"Dang it, Doc!" I said. "That hurts."

"You should have thought about that before you got in that fist fight," he said.

"Well, can you?"

"Can I what?"

"Can you tell if it is blood on that sack?"

"I can look at it through my microscope and see if it compares to a known blood stain," he said. "I won't be able to tell if it is Bradshaw's blood, though."

He finished stitching my eye and turned to the book he had been reading, picked it up and thumbed through it.

"Right here," he said, showing me a page.

I looked at it and there was a picture of something that I didn't recognize. It looked like an ink stain to me.

"What am I looking at?"

"That picture is of a human blood cell," he said.

I looked at the title of the book. It was The *Photographic Review of Medicine and Surgery* (1870), by F. F. Muary and L.A. Duhring.

"So what you are saying is that you can compare the stain on that sack with this picture and determine that it is human blood?"

"Yes, I can tell if it is human blood," he said.

"But you won't be able to testify that it is Bradshaw's"

"No. I can't testify to that," he said. "I can offer an opinion, but that may not be good in a court of law."

I stood up and picked up my hat.

"Well, I guess we'll just have to wait and see what happens," I said.

"Yes, Charles." He closed the book and put it on his shelf. "Come back in a week and let me remove those sutures."

"OK, Doc," I said. "How much do I owe you?"

"A dollar," he said. "But pay me when you can."

I paid him and left.

CHAPTER 24

I was at Garret's office early, waiting for him to get there. As soon as he arrived I asked about the bag.

"You taking that bag to Doc this morning, Sheriff?"

"First thing," he said. "As soon as I have a cup of coffee."

We went in to his office and he poured water from a bucket into a pot and stirred the coals in a small stove.

"It'll take all day to make that coffee, Sheriff," I said. "I'll buy you a cup of coffee at the hotel if you'll get that bag to the Doc."

"I know how much this means to you, Merritt," he said. "OK. Just let me find something here. It's a form that the Doc has to sign." He ruffled through his desk drawer and finally stood upright and showed me the form.

"That's it?" I asked.

"Yep."

"Then let's get going."

We left his office and walked the short distance to the Doc's office. I was hoping that the Doc would be in, and not out on the town delivering a baby or splinting a broken arm or something.

We went in and saw Skinny Horse, sitting in a corner looking through the same book the Doc had shown me.

"Hello Skinny Horse," I said.

He looked up and smiled at me.

"Hello Skinny Cowboy," he laughed out loud, causing me to grin.

"Is Doc here?" Garrett asked.

"Be in soon," Skinny Horse said. "He's eating at hotel."

"Are you looking at the pictures in that book?"

"Me read." He said, smiling broadly. "Doc teach me White Man's letters."

"Oh come on, you can't read that book," I said, disbelieving.

He stood up and brought the open book to me, held it with one hand and pointed at a word.

"That word "medicine"" he said.

I looked. Sure enough he was right. It was medicine.

"What's the next one?" I asked.

"One word I know." He said. "Sun come up one day at a time. I learn one word one day. Today I learn another. Doc tell me I learn to read that way."

I was thinking that he would be a hundred and ten when he learned enough words to read that book, but then if that pleased him, I was happy for him.

"Come on, Sheriff," I said. "We'll meet Doc at the hotel and you can have your coffee there."

Doc was having a second cup of coffee when we got to the hotel dining room. Garrett gave him the bag and asked him to sign the slip of paper. Doc signed it, then asked,

"Why'd you bring that nasty bag in here where I'm eatin' my breakfast, Garrett? Aint you got any manners?"

"Sorry, Doc," Garrett said. "I just want to get on with this. I've got other things to do."

"Such as?"

"There's been a steady increase in cattle rustling over the past few months. Four ranchers have filed complaints that their herds are getting thinned by as much as a quarter. I've got lots of work to do."

"Rustlers? Sure it aint Indians, Sheriff?" I asked.

"It don't seem like it," the sheriff said. "I rode out to Gebhart's ranch and he showed me where some fence was cut. Tracks led back towards Yuma. Indians usually will steal one or two head at a time and head south, across the border."

"How far have you tracked them?" I asked.

"Near to McAllister's ranch. I can't go further than that, it's a two day ride from here and two back. I can't leave the town without law enforcement for longer than that. Of course if you'd agree to be deputized, I'd let you track them, Charles Merritt."

"Me?" I said.

"Yes you." Garrett looked me straight in the eye. "You don't have a job. If you keep hanging around that saloon gambling, you may be broke soon, or dead. In any case you'll never amount to a hill of beans if you don't stay out of there. I'm offering you a good paying job. Twenty five dollars a month. Steady work."

I thought about that for a while. He was right. I'd noticed that I'd been drinking too much whiskey and staying up too late every night playing poker. My winnings were starting to deplete. Luck is a flighty lady, and mine had began to spread its wings.

"Better take it, Charles," Doc said. "I can't think of anybody around here that I'd rather have as a deputy."

"All right, Sheriff," I said. "I'll be your deputy. Just one word though. When I find the man who killed Will, I might resign on the spot so I can put a bullet in him."

"I guess I'll just have to worry about that when it happens," he said. "Come back to the office with me and I'll swear you in and give you a badge."

CHAPTER 25

Early the next morning, with Paint loaded down carrying a week's supply of coffee, hard tack, beans and water, I headed for the McAllister ranch for the third time in less than a month. I knew every anthill on the trail by now and was looking forward to seeing Elizabeth once again.

The sheriff had told me where to look for the track he had found, near a wash on the northeast side of the ranch, near a small grove of ironwood trees. I figured I'd get near the ranch by dark, camp overnight at the trees, and examine the area the next day before riding in to see the McAllisters.

I rode steadily, Paint picking his way along the trail with the agility of a mountain lion, me swaying with the motion and, at times, dozing off to dream of Elizabeth. I had the most wonderful dream. The two of us were boarding the train west, headed into the sun, me in a new suit, new boots and a new hat, Elizabeth in the peach colored dress I'd bought for her.

When I awoke I wondered why I hadn't brought that dress with me so I could give it to her.

Near dark I found the ironwood grove and made camp, built a small fire, made coffee and warmed some beans. As I sat eating I looked south towards the McAllister ranch and could see a barbed wire fence stretching from east to west across the landscape. Garrett was right, the grove was near the McAllister place.

There was just enough daylight left to wander around the ironwood grove a little, so I rolled one, lit it, and walked to the north edge of the grove and examined the ground there. I saw a whole bunch of cattle prints and one or two tracks that were made by horses. At first I figured that the horse prints were made by wild horses until I knelt and looked close. They were made by shod horses. One set showed a wide hoof, with a peculiar mark near the front of it. That would be the right rear hoof of a large horse, I thought.

The mark was where the shoe had bent near the front, making the track deeper on one side than the other. It was something that I had seen happen many times, a galloping horse would clip a rock with a hoof, hard enough to make a bend in the shoe on that hoof. A good horseman checks his horse's hooves regularly to make sure that none are split, that the shoes are secured and no nails are missing.

The hoof that had left that particular mark would soon start to grow around the shoe where it had indented into the hoof. If not removed and repaired, the horse would develop an abscessed hoof and eventually start to limp. No good horseman would ever let his horse go lame from a damaged shoe.

One thing that I knew for sure. Indians had not been driving this herd. Indians seldom if ever shoe a horse.

I walked back to the camp site and poured another cup of coffee, threw the cigarette butt in the fire and sat down. In the distance I could hear a coyote howl. Closer up I could hear night sounds, crickets and critters.

I laid my bedroll out, took my boots off and stretched out. Paint made a slight whinnying noise and reminded me that he wanted to eat too, so I got up and gave him a double handful of oats from a feed bag, and gathered some sage grass for his midnight snack.

Moments later I was sound asleep.

When I woke up my first thought was how I was going to get Paint through that barbed wire fence so I could ride to the McAllister ranch house. I had no idea how far the fence stretched west, but it had been at least eight or nine miles back to the east when I turned off of the main trail and started following the fence line north. I didn't want to circle back the way I came if I could help it.

I decided to ride the fence line west a ways to see if there was a gate or an opening. It didn't take long to find it. The track of the herd that I'd seen led me right to it. The barbed wire had been cut, the cattle driven through, then the wire had been spliced.

I wondered momentarily if I was seeing right. If the tracks I'd picked up were the same ones Garrett had followed from just north of Tucson, then why were these cattle being herded on to McAllister's property? It didn't make a bit of sense. Was McAllister a rustler? I wouldn't believe that one if a preacher told it to me.

I unwound the spliced wire, led Paint through, then wound the spliced wire back in place, mounted up and headed south towards the ranch house. If I was lucky, I'd get there in time for breakfast.

CHAPTER 26

I tied Paint to a rail near the bunkhouse and joined the group of cowboys headed for the Chuck Wagon. Baked beans and corn bread was the morning meal, and I'd had beans the night before, but I was hungry and ate heartily. The foreman welcomed me, asked how I'd been and if I'd found Will's killer yet.

When I turned the top of my shirt inside out and showed him my badge, he got a serious look on his face.

"What's a deputy doing out here? Are you looking for outlaws or in-laws?" He laughed.

"I was sent by Garrett. He trailed a herd of stolen cattle to an ironwood grove north east of here, and I picked up the trail and they headed west a ways."

"West? Wasn't Indians was it?"

"No," I said. "The herd was driven onto McAllister's ranch. Barbed wire had been clipped a mile or so from the ironwood grove. Herd went through right there."

"This ranch? What are you saying, Charles? McAllister aint got any stolen cattle here."

It was at about that moment when McAllister himself walked towards the table on crutches made by Skinny Horse. He was still pale looking, but was handling the loss of his leg with skill that told me he hadn't spent much time laying around moaning about it.

"What stolen cattle are you talking about?" he asked.

Then he recognized me and a smile broke out on his face.

"Well, danged if it ain't Charles Merritt. What brings you out here, Charles? I hope you've come to see Elizabeth. She's been quiet as a church mouse since you left."

"Hello, Mr. McAllister," I said.

"Charles just told me he tracked some stolen cattle onto your property, Sam."

"My property?" Sam said, a look of astonishment spread across his face, replacing the smile.

"Yep." I said. "I've been deputized by Garrett to try to find a herd stolen north of Tucson. He tracked them as far as that ironwood grove near here. I tracked them from there to a cut in your fence line. They were driven through on to your place, Mr. McAllister."

"The hell you say," he said.

"I don't know what to think about that," I told him. "I'm sure you don't have time to send your boys to Tucson to steal cattle."

"My hands ain't stole nothing," he said, frowning and raising his voice.

"No, I don't think they did," I said. "I've just got to ask some questions, and then I'll be on my way. Thank you for breakfast, Sam."

"You ain't going anywhere till you've talked to Elizabeth," he said. "Jim, go fetch Elizabeth out here. I want her to here Charles Merritt's accusations.'

"Now hold on, Sam," I said, hastily. "I'm not accusing anyone of anything. I saw what I saw and I'll be glad to show you what I'm talking about."

Jim got up and headed for the house. I looked up and saw that Elizabeth had just opened the kitchen door and was standing on the porch looking as beautiful as a sunrise over purple sage brush. My heart skipped about four beats just looking at her.

I saw Jim gesturing to her, his lips moving. She glanced at me as he talked, then headed towards the table, picking up her skirt hem to keep it out of the dust.

"Why are you here, Charles Merritt? Do you understand what you are implying? My father's ranch will not harbor thieves, and we are not going to listen to that nonsense!"

"Hello, Elizabeth," I stammered. "I'm not implying anything. I just rode in to have a bite with your foreman and ask a few questions."

"That's the only reason you're here?" she said, a look of disdain spreading across her pretty face.

"Well, I wanted to see you again, too," I said, meekly.

"That's a fine way to come to see me, bringing bad news about stolen cattle found on my Dad's ranch!"

"I ain't found any yet," I said, hastily.

"You won't either," she said. "We are not cattle thieves, Charles Merritt. I'll thank you to just get back on that paint horse of yours and ride back to Tucson and tell Garrett we don't harbor cattle thieves here at McAllister."

"Simmer down, honey," Sam McAllister said, looking at my crestfallen face. I felt like a little kid who had just watched his favorite girl rip up a valentine he'd given her.

"I'm sorry, Daddy," she said. "I'll leave this to you."

She turned and picked up her skirt again and walked back to the porch. I thought I heard dishes rattling in the kitchen when she slammed the door. My dreams of boarding a train and heading off into the sun were fading fast.

"Charles, I won't be as harsh as Elizabeth. I know you've told me the truth. You can stay and ask all the questions you want, but I don't think you'll find any stolen cattle here. Every head of cattle on my place carries my brand. It's a big "M" a little "c" and a big "A". You've probably seen it."

"Yes, sir." I said.

"If you find any cattle on my ranch with a different brand, you come and tell me. I'll return them to their rightful owner."

He leaned on his crutches and spun his good leg around and hobbled back towards the kitchen. The door didn't slam when he went in.

"What kind of questions do you have for me, Charlie?" Jim asked.

"You're the foreman, Jim," I said. "You direct the activities of this establishment. Do you know of any of your hands who've been unaccounted for recently? Any that you might have thought stayed in town, or got drunk and just didn't come back when they were supposed to?"

"Now that you mention it, I had two cowboys that were gone a day longer than they should have been," he said. My ears were attuned quickly.

"Who were they? Did they say where they'd been?"

"I'm going to tell you, but you've got to promise me you ain't going to start another fight."

"Start a fight….." I thought for a minute. He must be talking about Younger. "Hold on, Jim. First, I didn't start that fight. Second, If Younger went absent a day or two, I'm going to talk to him, whether you want me to or not. You got that?"

"Now you hold on, Charles." he said. "Don't get your bowels in an uproar. Yes, it was Younger, and a fella by the name of Clayton Roper. Clayton is the one you had the tiff with the day we chased them renegades off. You shot part of the man's thumb off, remember?"

"Oh," I said

"You've been into it with both of those men, and I just want you to walk softly when you go asking questions. I don't need any more fights, ain't got time to break them up."

"OK, Jim. I promise there won't be any fights, on my part. But I can't help what somebody else might do."

"Just be careful," he said. "I've taken a liking to you, Charles Merritt. I'd hate to see anything bad happen to you."

CHAPTER 27

Roper and Younger were both in the bunkhouse when I went in. Neither one of them spoke, so I started it up.

"Just the two cowboys I'm looking for," I said. "I'd like to ask you boys some questions, if you don't mind."

Roper looked at Younger, then looked at the floor of the bunkhouse like he was getting sick to his stomach or something.

"What kind of questions, and who gave you the authority to ask them?" Younger said.

"Garrett deputized me," I said. "I would like to know where you two fellers were the day that Jim said you didn't return to the ranch when you were supposed to."

"We got drunk in Tucson and spent the night there," Younger said.

"Where'd you sleep?" I asked.

"That ain't none of your damned business, Merritt," Roper said, his eyes sending death rays towards me. His right hand was encased in a dirty bandage. "You aint got no right to pry into our private lives."

I opened my shirt and showed them the badge pinned on the inside.

"You're right," I told him. " I don't have the right. But the Sheriff does, and I represent him. Now where'd you boys stay that night?"

"In the hotel," Younger said quickly. "We had a little too much to drink. Aint no law against that, is there?"

He looked at me with a dark stare that would have made Roper's look like a Sunday school teacher's.

"By the way, where's your horses?" I said, changing the tactics.

"Mine's tied up by the corral gate," Younger said. "You'll recognize it, I'm sure, since you claim it's your horse."

"Jim lets you ride that roan?" I asked, disbelieving.

"Jim ain't got nothing to say about it," he said, looking straight in my eyes. "I bought that horse from McAllister. It's my horse now, no matter who broke it."

I swallowed hard. It was bad news that he'd bought the horse I broke. I figured that the law of the plains was that whoever broke a horse owned it. I could see his point, though. Technically the horse belonged to McAllister, and if he'd bought it, now it was his.

"Where's that nag you ride, Roper?" I said.

"It's in the corral. I ain't saddled it yet."

"I'll just have a look then," I said. "I hope you fellers are telling me the truth. If I find out you lied, it's going to be hard on both of you."

"Lying ain't against the law," Roper said.

"Stealing cattle is," I told him.

"You calling us rustlers?" Younger said, his chin raising slightly and his gun hand dropping to his side.

"I ain't calling you anything, except a horse thief," I told him, watching his eyes. Then I remembered what Jim had told me. Don't start any fights.

"I told you, I bought that horse, it's mine now."

"Have it your way," I said, and turned on my heels and walked out of the bunkhouse.

I found the roan tied to the corral's top rail. I was particularly interested in its feet. I picked up one leg at a time, inspected the forelock and the shoe, then dropped it. The roan sidled away from me and snorted. He still didn't like me much, and I was cautious not to get kicked. Satisfied that none of the shoes matched the print I'd seen, I opened the corral gate and walked slowly to a dapple gray that I knew Roper was riding.

It didn't take me long to find what I was looking for. The right rear hoof on Roper's horse had a bent shoe. The hoof was bigger than most horses hoofs, the shoe was bent just like the print showed. I held the horse's hoof up long enough to see that an infection had started to spread where the bent shoe had penetrated the hoof.

I dropped the leg and walked out of the corral and towards the table where Jim still sat drinking his coffee.

"It seems like one of the cowboys who drove that herd on this ranch is employed here," I said.

"What? You don't say!" Jim sputtered.

"Roper's horse has a bent shoe on the right rear. It matches prints I found where the fence had been cut and cattle driven through. I'd like to ride out and see if I can find those cattle here on McAllister's ranch."

"If Roper's a rustler, he did it on his own, Charles," Jim said. "You know McAllister wouldn't tolerate somebody stealing cattle."

"I only know what I saw with my own eyes, Jim. It looked like two riders herded stolen cattle to the back fence of McAllister's, cut the fence, drove the cattle through, then patched the fence. One of those riders was Roper, by the looks of his horse. He won't ride that horse much longer, it'll go lame. The shoe is bent into the hoof and an infection has started."

"What kind of low-life would let that happen to his horse?" Jim said.

"Maybe a cattle rustler?" I said.

"You'll need more proof than that," Jim said. "These cowboys are all over this ranch, and outside the fences too. If there's prints in the dirt, that don't prove anything. I guess you know that, though."

"It doesn't prove they stole the herd," I said, "But it doesn't take much of a tracker to figure out who drove them cattle on to McAllister."

"Just tread easy, Charles," Jim said. "I'd hate to see you tangle with Roper again. And he's the kind that might not give you a warning."

"I'll be careful," I said. "I'm going to tell McAllister what I found, though. I'll leave here on a peaceful note, at least with those two, Roper and Younger. Not so sure about Elizabeth, though."

"I figured you might have an eye for that girl, Charles. Let me tell you, she's a hellcat. She don't take any guff off of anyone."

"I know that," I said. "I'll be careful with her too."

I turned away from the table and headed for the kitchen door.

CHAPTER 28

Sam McAllister sat and listened to me tell about the broken shoe, the tracks, and finding that Roper's horse had a matching broken shoe on its right rear hoof. He grimaced and put both hands on the arms of his kitchen chair.

Elizabeth stood quietly near the stove listening. When I had finished she walked to the chair where her father sat and put both hands on his shoulders.

"What do you think Roper is up to, Dad?"

"I don't know, Honey," he said. "I'll not say anything to him though until Charles finishes his investigation. I'm sure that those cattle are long since gone, if they were ever on this place, as Charles thinks."

"Oh they were here all right," I said, glancing at Elizabeth. "I'm sorry to bring news like this to your house, Sir. It's a part of the reason I almost didn't take this job."

"Part of the reason?" McAllister asked.

"Yes, Sir."

"What's the rest of the reason?"

"Well, I thought Elizabeth might have told you," I said. "I'm waiting trial for train robbery in Tucson."

"Elizabeth?" he said, looking at his daughter.

"I didn't think it mattered, Dad," she said. "I don't think they will ever find Charles guilty of train robbery. Why would Garrett hire him if he thought Charles had robbed a train. No-one believes he is guilty."

"That's why Garrett came here and got you?" McAllister asked, turning back to me.

"Yes, Sir," I said. "It's a long story."

"Tell me," he said.

I began with Will getting sick, the long ride south to put him on the train, finding Will's body with the note and the money gone. The conductor who had told me he didn't shoot Will. The damned bandana handkerchief. The bag of money tossed into my hands.

"So that was just a coincidence?"

"A bad set of circumstances," I said. "Then when I thought I'd clear myself by giving back the money, someone shot the one friend I'd made in town and stole the money. Now, though, a man is in jail in Tucson. He had a bag like the one the train money was in, with blood on it. Doc says he can testify that it is human blood, but not that it was the livery owner's blood."

"Bradshaw's dead?" McAllister said. "You didn't tell me any of this, Elizabeth. Would you like to explain yourself?"

"Dad, I took the gold that Mother left me and bailed Charles out of jail. I didn't want you to know that I'd done that, so I never told you any of what happened. You were ill and I didn't want to upset you."

"That gold is for your dowry, Elizabeth!" McAllister said, and then he turned to me. "I hope you can pay Elizabeth back, Charles Merritt."

"He's paid me back already, Dad," Elizabeth said. "I've put the gold back in my cedar chest."

"See that it stays there!" He said. "As much as I admire this young man, I don't know if I'd go so far as to bail him out of jail. What is there between the two of you?"

Elizabeth blushed and I felt my face growing red. Neither of us spoke.

"Well?" he said.

"Charles helped me save your life, Dad," she finally spoke. "I felt I owed him something. I didn't believe that he had robbed a train."

He glanced at me. I didn't have any idea at all what to say, or even if I should say anything.

He looked at me sternly for several seconds, then turned on his crutch and walked towards the door.

"Come, Charles," he said. "I want to talk to Roper."

When we found Roper he was just getting ready to mount his horse. McAllister hollered at him.

"Hold on a minute!" he said.

Roper stood next to the horse.

"What is it, boss?" he said.

"I'd like to see that horse's right back foot if you'd lift it."

Roper glanced at me, then back at McAllister.

"What's this tinhorn telling you about my horse?"

"Never mind, Roper. Just lift that hoof like I asked you to."

Roper lifted the horse's hoof and McAllister's face showed a tint of surprise.

He turned and looked at me.

"Take a look at this, Charles."

I looked. The right rear horseshoe had been replaced. The one on the horses hoof now was straight, no bend in it all. The hoof had been trimmed neatly.

Some time in the past thirty minutes since I had looked at it, someone had removed the bent shoe, trimmed the hoof neatly and put on a new shoe. I turned my back on the horse, spread my legs and backed up to where I could hold the horses hoof up myself.

"Let's have a closer look," I said.

I took the hoof in my hands, raised it and looked carefully. The hoof had been trimmed, but signs of infection in the forelock still showed. A thin line of dark stain ran down the side. I bent and smelled of the hoof. Turpentine.

"This shoe was changed within the last half an hour," I said. "The one that was on here was bent, you can see where the forelock has an infection. I can smell turpentine where it has been treated recently."

"Did you change the shoe on this horse's hoof, Roper?"

"Yeah, Boss. But it wasn't bent. My horse backed into a cactus and had a cactus thorn in its leg. I treated it with turpentine and removed the shoe to make sure there weren't any cactus spines under it. Then I put the shoe back on."

"He's lying, Sir." I said, dropping the hoof and standing up quickly.

Roper stepped back.

"I don't want any trouble, Boss," he said. "But if you let this tinhorn call me a liar again, I'm going to box his ears for him."

"You aint boxin' anyone's ears, Roper." a voice said.

I turned and looked. It was Jim.

"You are a liar!" Jim said. "I was watching you from the far side of that barn and I saw you take a shoe off this horse, rub some turpentine on the horse's leg, trim the hoof and put on a different shoe. This is the one you took off."

He raised his right hand and held it out. It held the bent shoe I'd seen on the horse earlier.

"Well maybe I did put a new shoe on it," Roper said.

"Get your gear and get off of my place," McAllister said. "A man that lies to me can't work for me."

Roper's face turned a shade between purple and red, he turned and grabbed the horse's reins and led it towards the bunkhouse.

"Are you going to arrest him?" Jim asked me.

"No, I don't have anything except my word about the hoof prints. I'll ask around Tucson about where that pair were the night the cattle were stolen. If they lied to me, I'll find out. Then I'll arrest both of them."

McAllister had started back to the ranch house kitchen.

I caught up with him.

"I'm riding out," I said. "I'm sorry to bring this to you, but I thought you should know."

"Well, Charles, you do what you need to do. I think you know that this ranch wouldn't stand for cattle rustlin'. I won't keep hands that break the law, either."

"Will you say goodbye to Elizabeth for me?"

"You'd best do that job for yourself, Charles Merritt," he said.

I followed him into the house and stood with my hat in my hand as he walked through the kitchen. Elizabeth showed up a few seconds later and closed the door behind her.

"Dad said you wanted to tell me something."

"I just wanted to bid you farewell for now," I said. "I have to ride. If you'll allow me, I'll come back to see you soon."

"I'd like that," she said.

I stepped close to her and took her hands in mine.

"Elizabeth….."

"Don't say anything yet," she said. "Goodbye, Charles. I hope you won't stay gone long."

I dropped her hands and turned to the door. As I went out I heard her say something that I didn't understand. I turned and looked at her.

"Beg pardon?"

"I said, be careful, Charles. I want you to come back to see me soon."

She stood there looking so danged beautiful it hurt. I wanted to go back and take her in my arms and give her a hug and kiss those full, pouting lips, but something in her eyes was telling me that the time for that wasn't yet here.

"I'll be back soon, I promise," I said.

CHAPTER 29

I rode back to the place where I'd found the tracks leading on to the property and followed them for a short way where I found sign indicating that the small herd had been bedded down. There were two holes in the ground where posts might have been, about 20 yards apart and about 20 yards from the barbed wire fence.

A temporary corral, I guessed. Someone had set two posts, strung either a rope or a string of wire, just to hold the rustled cattle for a night or so before being moved. It didn't take me long to find the place in the fence that had been cut and then spliced. That's where they took them back off of McAllister's property, I thought.

I wondered why the rustlers had brought the herd on to McAllister in the first place, then I realized that grazing them on the north side of the little barranca might have been hard to do. There was little grass on that side. And, too, with the small rustled herd inside McAllister's fences, anyone who passed by and saw them wouldn't get curious.

I followed the trail almost due east, gradually angling away from McAllister's fence line and heading into more barren, dry countryside, starting to climb into the foothills. They led up a dry gulch as I climbed. I knew the bottom of the gulch opened into the creek that ran east and west behind the McAllister ranch. I rode steadily, giving Paint his head and relaxing in the saddle. The sign that the small herd left was easy to read and I didn't have to dismount to follow it.

By the time the sun was shining mostly on my right side I knew I was headed south, but I knew that by now I was far enough east that I'd miss the ranch by several miles. The railroad that ran through Tucson would be another days ride from there. The terrain gradually sloped down, away from the foothills and towards the desert, inhabited only by rattlers and lizards.

At twilight I reined Paint to a stop and dismounted, removed the saddle and blanket and looped the reins a few times around a big rock. I made a small fire and fixed coffee, chewed on a piece of dried beef, and washed down a hardtack biscuit with the coffee.

The stars spread themselves out above me on a blanket of black velvet. If a man paid no mind to the discomforts of being hungry, tired and smelling of horse sweat and his own odors, needing the warmth of a kitchen stove on his back, the sounds of human voices instead of coyotes, the desert was a beautiful place to be. There was a solitude that seeped into a man's soul and made him realize that he was insignificant in the plan God made when He made the heavens and the earth.

My thoughts drifted around in my head, first of Elizabeth and how beautiful she had been when I spoke to her last.

I thought of Will and the plans we had made. A lump of sorrow swelled in my throat and I had to take a sip of the lukewarm coffee to wash it down. It still rankled me that I hadn't found out who shot Will, and now I was off on a wild goose chase trying to catch some phantom cattle rustlers. I let it go after a while and stretched out on my bedroll, used Paint's saddle blanket for a pillow and slept.

I was up at first light, saddled Paint and drank what was left of the coffee without warming it. An hour's ride later I found a place where the herd had stopped. There were a lot of horse tracks around the area, two of them were shod and had been part of the sign I had followed to this point. Eight or more, to the best of my judgment, were unshod horses. Indians. The tracks were evenly spaced and not deep in the sand. That told me that the Indians had not rode hard in and snatched the cattle away. No, they had met the two men who had driven the cattle and peacefully took control of them.

Either the rustlers were paying the Indians to take the cattle to another place, or the Indians were paying for the cattle and reselling them or using them for food. I rode in a big circle around the spot, letting Paint drift further away on each sweep. I didn't find any sign of a war party camp. No dead fires, no campsites, no sign of slaughtered cattle. It was my guess that the Indians were being paid to move the cattle further south.

Late that afternoon I got to the railroad track. There was a small watering hole nearby and a few scraggly willows around it. I let Paint drink while I studied the site. The tracks around the watering hole showed me that the 20 or so head of cattle I had been trailing had all been watered here. Unshod horse tracks said that the Indians had watered their horses here too. The problem was that the cattle tracks stopped at the railroad track.

No sign of cattle tracks anywhere. The unshod horse tracks continued south past the railroad bed, but the cattle had to have been loaded on a car and hauled away. Cows don't fly, I told myself, so that was the only answer.

I couldn't track the Indians without putting myself in danger. I had a choice to make, the long ride back to McAllister's or wait for the east bound train and pay passage back towards Tucson, or ride back to Tucson. The first choice would let me see Elizabeth again, the second would get me back to make my report to the sheriff faster, the third would be a long hard ride with no reward except a sore hind end and not much to eat.

I chose the second option. As much as I wanted to see Elizabeth, I needed to get on with my own personal business of finding Will's killer. I made camp and settled down to wait for the East bound train.

The noise of the train startled me from an afternoon nap in the shade of a group of cactus. I heard it long before I saw the smoke from it. When there is nothing but silence all around you, you will hear sounds that are far away. I got up fast and walked the twenty yards to the track and started waving my hands, holding my hat in one of them. By that time I could see the smoke from the engine. With any luck the engineer would see me and start applying the brakes soon enough so that I wouldn't have to walk far in the heat to reach the train after it stopped.

I was lucky.

The train had just climbed a grade and was already slowing when the engineer spotted me. He got it stopped less than a hundred yards from my spot. I had Paint saddled and rode the short distance to the passenger car. I didn't recognize the conductor but paid my fare and got Paint settled in a cattle car. I hoped that I would be reimbursed for travel.

Once the train was moving again I roamed around asking questions of the crew members about the cattle that had been boarded on the West bound train. None of them had been on that train and knew nothing of importance. The engineer was the same one who had given me a tour of the engine. He said he'd heard of a small herd of cattle being transported to Yuma, but had no details.

The passenger car was almost empty; a salesman of some sort, an older woman with two small children, and myself. I had plenty of room so I stretched out across a couple of seats and snoozed.

CHAPTER 30

The train was just pulling in to Tucson when I woke up. I could see a bunch of people milling around the station as they always did when a train stopped, wondering who was getting on or getting off. Somebody was always coming or going.

I got off. After retrieving Paint from the cattle car, I walked, leading the horse, down to the saloon. My throat was dry and I needed a whiskey to ease the jumble in my mind.

I had dreamed of Will and how we had rode west, looking for our dreams. I dreamed about building the small spread, about working our butts off to get a herd started, about lonesome nights and endless days, hunger and hard work.

Now I was thinking of one thing. Find Will's killer and put a slug in him.

The saloon door swung wide as I pushed through it into the dim interior. The afternoon sun had already passed the roof of the board sidewalk and there was little light in the interior of the drinking place.

The young bartender was on duty and poured me one before I even got to the bar. I reached for my silver but he pushed the drink towards me and said, "On me, Merritt."

"Thanks," I said. "What makes you so generous today?"

"I'm glad to see you back, that's all," he said.

"Well I'm glad to be back."

"Garrett has been out of town for three days and I've had to raise the shotgun twice to keep peace in here. I figure you'll settle things down a bit as soon as word gets around that you're back."

"Don't count on it," I said. I had work to do and that might mean I wouldn't have much time to socialize in the saloon.

"Anything else new?" I asked.

"They've set the date for your trial," he said.

"When?"

"Let's see, I believe it's a week from today."

"I wish they would have told me before I left town, I don't know if I'm ready to stand trial."

"You'll be fine," he said. "Doc says that the blood on that sack was definitely human and he'll testify to that. Garrett said he'll put in a word for you, and I heard that Dressler is going to testify on your behalf too."

"Dressler?" I asked, surprised. "What's he know that I don't?"

"You'd have to ask him," he said.

"I will, thank ye," I said and downed the drink. "If you see him, tell him I'm looking for him, will you?"

"Sure thing, deputy," he said, smiling.

I walked to the hotel and paid for a bath, hoping to clean up in peace without the temptation of the clerk. It was an older woman who took my bath money and handed me a towel.

I had washed and was standing up in the lukewarm water of the tub when I heard a noise behind me. I turned instinctively towards the sound just in time to see a man with a bandana over his face, arm extended, pointing a gun at me.

I dropped to my haunches as the gun roared. Somewhere behind me and to my right I heard the slug hit the wall, as I tumbled out of the tub, dragging my holster from the clothes rack. His second shot hit the tub I'd just been in, water spurted out through the hole. I hit the floor hard, pried the gun from the holster and fired at the figure I could barely see through the smoke from his gun.

His arm jerked up and his third shot hit the ceiling over my head. Plaster rained down on me as he fell backwards, hit hard and then rolled towards the door. My second shot busted his head open like it was a ripe watermelon.

The old woman who had sold me the bath came running into the room. I grabbed the towel and held in front of me with one hand, my smoking revolver in the other. She saw the body, brains and blood on the floor and screamed, running back towards the lobby.

I pulled on my pants and walked to the body. I didn't have any idea who would want to bushwhack me until I pulled the bandana away from the bloody face. It was Roper.

CHAPTER 31

Dressler was the next person to enter the room.

"What the hell's going on in here?" He asked.

"I've just killed a man," I said. "He was trying to kill me, but I guess I'm a bit faster than he was. His shots missed, mine didn't."

"I see that," he said. "Who is he?"

"A cowboy that I had a run in with at McAllister's ranch. He was one of my suspects in a rustling gang. I found hoof prints of his horse at a place where rustled cattle had been grazed."

"Prints don't mean he's a rustler," Dressler said. "They could have been made anytime."

"Why'd he try to kill me?" I asked.

"Don't know," Dressler replied. "Maybe he had another reason. You said you had a run in with him."

"I reckon it's because of what I had found out about the rustling gang that's been working ranches around here."

I told him about finding the tracks and confronting Roper at McAllister's, how McAllister had fired Roper and chased him off of his place.

"He might have just had a bone to pick with you for getting him fired, not because of any rustling activities."

"Yeah, well I think he was part of it. I also think that the reason he tried to kill me is to stop me from finding out who is responsible for the rest of it."

"You may be right," Dressler said.

By that time a few more people had stuck their heads through the door into the bathtub room and now and then someone would mutter something about the body.

A man came in with a box like contraption on three legs, set it up, held a pan of powder up over his head and took a picture of the dead man. I'd only seen a half a dozen pictures taken in my life and at first I didn't realize what he was doing until it was too late, and he left, carrying the camera with him. He was back within minutes, writing something on a tablet. He began firing questions at me faster than I had drawn and fired my gun.

"Why'd you kill him, Mr. Merritt?"

I yelled at him to get the hell out and don't come back. Dressler looked grim and retreated into the lobby of the hotel.

I finished dressing and found him waiting for me.

"You'll be the headline in every newspaper in Arizona, Charlie."

"Can't be helped," I said. "I'd rather be the headline than the deadline."

He laughed at that.

"Problem is every punk kid with a gun will be thinking that if he kills Charlie Merritt he'll be famous and have his picture in the newspapers."

"I'd hate that," I said. "I don't hanker to have to kill a bunch of kids who want to be famous. I wonder if Garret feels that way?"

"You'd have to ask him," Dressler said. "I felt that way for a while."

"Who'd you kill?" I asked.

"You don't want to know, Charles. If I told you, I'd have to kill you." He chuckled.

"I guess I'd better get over to the office and write up what happened," I said.

"That'd be a good idea, you know that newspaper will be full of speculation about the whole deal."

I pulled my dirty hat down over my eyes and walked out into the bright sunlight. People walking along the dusty street froze and stared at me. I'd been a gunslinger for only a few minutes and already I hated it; I don't like being stared at. I was wondering what Elizabeth would think when she got a copy of the paper. As far as I was concerned it didn't make a damned bit of difference what anyone else thought, but I didn't want Elizabeth to think of me as a gunslinger.

I figured that the shooting wouldn't set to well with a jury at my train robbing trial either, but that couldn't be helped. I'd return the money and the way I figured it, I'd be exonerated and get that behind me. One thing that still bothered me, though, was the part that the train played in the cattle rustling operation. Someone had to be on that west bound train, know the water stops, and pay the rustlers or Injuns for the cattle, load them into cars, then sell them on the other end. Whether that person knew he was buying rustled cattle or not was another thing, but I thought that if someone buys cattle off of Injuns, they must have some inkling that the cattle weren't raised by Injuns.

With that in mind I sat down at the Sheriff's desk, took a paper and pencil and started writing out what had happened at the hotel. The entire scene only took one page and I finished it in just a few minutes. Then I wrote a two page report on what I had found out on my trip. Garrett would know everything I had done after reading it.

Just as I finished writing and put the papers in Garrett's desk, young Ted Bradshaw, the son of the late blacksmith, walked into the office.

"Howdy, Ted," I said.

He was not a day older than 19 and built with the same blocky body and huge arms that his father had. His hands were big and strong.

He held his right hand out, fist clenched and said,

"Look at this, Sheriff."

I looked as he slowly uncurled his fingers from around my grandfather's gold watch.

CHAPTER 32

I jumped almost straight up out of the chair.

"Where'd you get that, Ted?"

"I was preparing that fella you shot for burial and found it in his pocket. It's got your name on it, so I figured it must be yours."

I took the watch from him and turned it over in my hand, pressed the button on the top and the lid opened to reveal the name "Charles Merritt" engraved on the inside, along with "1798", the year my grandpa was born.

Ted stood there shifting from one foot to the other, a grin on his face.

"It is your watch, aint it Charlie?"

"Well, technically it aint mine," I said. "I gave it to a train conductor for passage. But until I find out how that bushwhacking Roper got his hands on it, I'll take care of it."

"I remember you telling that to my Dad before he was killed." Ted said. "I hope the jury finds you innocent and that gunslinger Blacky guilty of killing Dad."

I glanced at the cell where Blacky was standing near the bars watching and listening to us. It seemed to me that his face paled a little. I'd bet he had something to do with the watch and Will's death. But my immediate task would be to find out what Chester Peak had to say about the watch.

"Can you take charge of this office for a day until Garrett gets back?" I asked.

"Sure, Charlie," he said. "I've got my younger brother to watch the livery. Will you deputize me?"

"I don't have that authority, Ted. I'll give you the keys to the cell and you can feed the prisoner. Get the food from the hotel. If anyone tries to break him out, shoot them with that 12 gauge hanging there." I pointed to the old shotgun hanging on the wall.

"It'll be all right, Charlie," he said. "Where you off to?"

"I'm riding east. I've got some questions for a fat railroad conductor and I want some better answers this time."

I left the office and walked to the livery, saddled Paint and rode back to the general store, bought some supplies and filled up my canteen at the saloon and added a pint of rotgut whiskey.

It was still early in the afternoon and I wanted to catch the train before it got to town. I didn't need a bunch of witnesses to watch me rough up a fat conductor, and I wanted to get him off to himself so he would answer my questions truthfully. Problem was, I really didn't know what I was going to ask him for sure.

One thing I figured to ask was how a cow rustling bushwhacker got a hold of my watch.

CHAPTER 33

I rode to the water tank on the railroad line. After the long ride I was still angry. I remembered that Chester Peak had told me he had got to feeling bad about taking my grandpa's watch and had put it in Will's pocket. If that was true, whoever shot Will probably took the watch.

And Roper had been carrying that watch when he tried to bushwhack me while I was taking a bath.

I knew the schedule of the train, and it would be coming soon.

My trip had another purpose. I had to be careful, though, to get back to Tucson before my trial date.

I would ride on to my ranch and check on things, then I'd ride to Randy Flockman's ranch and talk to him about any cattle he'd had stolen, and any changes of his cow pokes. Cowboys have a way of quitting one place and hiring on at another every once in a while. It could be something as simple as too much salt in the grub, an unfriendly foreman, or just a wanderlust in the cow puncher that makes them move on, but I would ask about recent ranch hands that had quit.

First things first, though, I wanted to talk to Chester Peak.

As luck would have it, the train arrived at the water tank an hour after I did, and Chester Peak was on board. I said hello to the engineer who had taught me a little about trains, then walked through the open doors to the passenger compartment where I found Chester.

"Good morning, Chester," I said.

He had been reading a newspaper and looked up at me with a startled look.

"I was just reading about you," he said, and handed me the paper. It was from a place in New Mexico called Las Cruces.

I looked it over and tossed it on the seat beside him. It had a bunch of garbage in the story about how I'd shot a man while laying on the floor of a bath room naked as a jaybird. How they'd got that story so fast was a mystery to me. It must have been telegraphed from Tucson.

"Never mind me," I said. "I want to know who has been selling cattle to someone on this Westbound train, and who's been buying those cows."

"That would be me," he said, easily, as if there was no big secret about it.

"You?"

"Yep. I buy a few head from Injuns about every third trip I make west. Then I sell them at Yuma for a dollar or two more per head than I pay."

"Do you know where those cattle come from?"

"From the Injuns," he said, as calm as could be.

"You nitwit, Chester," I said. "Those are stolen cattle. Don't you know Apaches don't raise cattle on their own? Did you ever check any of the brands?"

"Why no," he said. "I just thought the Injuns wanted to make a little money for whiskey, so they were rounding up strays and selling them."

I looked at him long and cold, shook my head and thought to myself that no one could be that dumb. But for some reason I believed him.

"One more thing," I said. "You told me that you got to feeling bad about my gold watch and you put it in Will's pocket. Is that the truth or are you lying to me?"

He quickly looked at the floor, then out the window of the car. Sweat popped out on his forehead, under the brim of his conductor's hat. I figured there was more to his story.

"Don't lie to me again, Chester. I just shot one man and another won't make that much difference."

"No, sir," he said.

"So tell me."

"I gave the watch for six head of cattle," he said, swallowing hard. "I was a little short when the Injuns brought them in, and I paid for them with the watch. One of the Injuns wanted it and convinced the others that it was a fair trade."

"Did any of those Injuns mention any of their names? Would you recognize any of them if you saw them again?"

"I'd know the one I gave the watch to," he said. "The others called him River Mouth."

"Anything else you want to tell me, Chester? And remember this, if I find out you're lying to me again, I'm going to take you apart, piece by piece. First I'll shoot your big ears off, then your nose, and then your fingers, unless I miss when I shoot at your nose."

"That's all I did! I swear it, Mr. Merritt."

I turned and walked away from him. What he had told me changed my plans. I'd ride out to see Randy some other time. For now, I was going to put Paint on this train and go back to Tucson. I would talk to Skinny Horse and see if he knew an Apache named River Mouth.

I paid for my passage back to Tucson and for a spot in the cattle car to put Paint. I made sure Paint had a bite of hay or two and walked back to the engine where I asked the engineer a few questions about Chester Peak's activity and the story he'd told me.

"I told that fat turd he was buying stolen cattle," the engineer said. "He said it didn't make a hoot to him as long as he could make a few dollars off it."

"That sounds like Chester," I said.

CHAPTER 34

By the time the train pulled in to Tucson I was sound asleep. The hissing of the air and the squeal of the wheels on the rails woke me. I stood up and stretched, then headed for the cattle car to get my horse.

I led Paint and carried the saddle to the livery. The youngest Bradshaw boy took the reins and saddle and I gave him fifty cents. He smiled and told me he'd take good care of Paint.

It had been a long ride, both to the water tank and back on the train, and I was wore out. I figured I'd get a swallow or two before talking to Skinny Horse. Mid afternoon he'd probably be deep in some medicine lecture from Doc and I didn't want to disturb them. Either that or they'd be out at some ranch patching somebody up or delivering a baby.

The saloon was half full of cowboys and merchants when I walked in. The young bartender motioned me over right away and smiled at me.

"Glad your back, Charles," he said. "You're lady friend was in here asking for you."

"What lady friend?"

"How many lady friends have you got, Charles?" He said, laughing.

"Not many," I said. "Are you talking about the girl who fills the bathtub at the hotel?"

"Hell no, Charlie," he said. "The pretty one from the ranch, you know, McAllister's daughter."

"Elizabeth?" I asked, not daring to believe it.

"Yep. That's the one! She said she wanted to talk to you."

"About what?" I asked.

"She didn't say, just that she needed to talk to you about something."

"Is she still in town?"

"Probably, Charlie. She was just in here not more than twenty minutes ago."

I dug out grandpa's gold watch and opened it. It was nearly 3 o:clock. She'd not leave this late to go back to the ranch, so she was probably staying the night in town, and the only hotel was the one where I had a room.

I practically tore the swinging doors off of their hinges running out of the place. I scared a few folks who were on the board walk and a horse shied away when I tore across the dirt street and headed towards the hotel.

I was thinking about the day I'd first met Elizabeth, running like a banshee trying to keep up with her, going for the Doc. When I reached the hotel I was out of breath. I noticed the McAllister buckboard with its horse tied to the rail. She was still here! I ran inside.

"Where's Elizabeth McAllister?" I almost yelled at the old lady behind the counter. I must have scared her too cause she jumped about a foot in the air. Maybe she thought I'd shot someone else.

"She's taking a bath, Mr. Merritt."

"Well how long has she been in there?" I asked, nodding towards the closed door to the bath room.

"Ten minutes or so, I'd guess" she said. "You'd best just simmer down and wait. Can I get you some water or something?"

"I'll be back," I said. I ran up the stairs to my room and changed my dirty shirt, poured some water in the porcelain bowl on the dresser, hauled out my razor and some soap and commenced to scrape a three day beard from my face. Then I dampened my hair and tried to arrange it so it didn't hang down around my eyes. I splashed on some witch hazel and hoped I didn't smell too bad.

I glanced at the mirror and was thinking that I was presentable enough when there came a knock on my door. I froze.

I didn't know who might be looking for me. In my racing imagination I envisioned Elizabeth on the other side of the door. Beautiful Elizabeth, fresh as a daisy after her bath, smelling like honeysuckles on a dew soaked morning. Eyes shining and lips pouting.

I opened the door with my right hand on my gun.

It was Sam McAllister, leaning on his crutches, a pipe clenched between his teeth.

"Hello Charles," he said through his teeth.

"Sam," I muttered, my imaginative dream shattered in a second.

"Can I come in? Just need a minute of your time."

"Well, come in," I said, stepping aside and closing the door behind him. He swung his way across the room on the crutches, and spun around and sat down in the only chair. I sat on the edge of the bed.

"What is it, Sam?"

"I need to ask you about Elizabeth, Charles."

"What about her?" I stuttered. "Is she OK?"

"Well she's fine, actually healthier and prettier than I've ever seen her since her momma died. That's what's got me worried."

"Why?"

"I think Elizabeth has taken a liking to you, Charles Merritt."

I blushed as bright as the afternoon sun peaking through the window. I glanced again at the mirror and saw my red face looking back at me, grinning like a possum.

I stood there silent, not knowing what to say, but grateful for the words I'd just heard. Sam took his pipe out of his mouth and looked me in the eye.

"What are your intentions regarding my daughter, Charles?"

"My intentions? Well, Sir, I think a lot of that would be whether or not Elizabeth agrees. I'd be mighty pleased to have Elizabeth be my wife, but I can't ask her to marry me with that train robbing trial facing me. After that's over and I'm found innocent, I will ask you for her hand."

"What about that story of you killing Roper in this hotel?"

"It's true, if that's what you mean," I said. "He tried to bushwhack me and I shot him."

"Why do you think Roper wanted you dead? Do you think that incident at my ranch had anything to do with him wanting to shoot you?"

"I think he was rustling cattle and knew that I was on to him. He may have been rustling cows back when I first rode to your place and fought the Injuns. We had words then."

"Well I ain't got no regrets about Roper, Charles. What I do think about is your reputation. I don't want Elizabeth to marry someone who has a reputation as a gun slinger. Every Tom, Dick and Harry will be testing you to build a reputation of their own."

"I'm no gunslinger, Sam." I said. "I've never killed anyone except Roper and a few Yankees when I was in the war, and an Injun or two."

"I've heard the story of your partner, Will. People say that you won't stop until you've gunned down the coyote that shot Will. Is that true?"

"I'm going to find Will's killer, Sam. What happens after that., I don't know. I guess either I'll bring him to justice for hanging or I'll shoot him if he tries to shoot me. I can't foretell the future. There's just one thing I am sure of. If I live long enough, I'll find the polecat that killed Will."

"I admire a man with determination, Charles," he said. "I hope you find Will's killer. But at the same time, I have to think of my daughter's future. Oh, she'll never want for anything, my ranch is hers if I die. But no amount of money can heal a broken heart, and if you two were married and some outlaw gunned you down, she'd likely curl up inside herself and slowly rot away to nothing."

I sat there silently. My heart was bubbling with the thought that Sam was telling me Elizabeth cared enough about me and that my life was important to her. At the same time, I could hear an undertone of regret in Sam's voice. He was thinking that I might not be the right man for his daughter if my destiny didn't change.

"I can't change the future any more than I can read it, Sam," I finally said, slowly. "I'll be good to Elizabeth and I'll cherish her, but if you want to hear that I won't ever kill another man or give up my pursuit of Will's killer, I can't promise that."

"Even if it means losing Elizabeth?"

"That would hurt me as much as her losing me might hurt her," I said. "If what you're asking is for me to leave Elizabeth alone, I can't do that either. I knew the day I laid eyes on her that I wanted to marry her. If she'll have me, I don't think there's much you can do to stop that."

"No," he said. "You are right. I can't stop you from loving Elizabeth. I can't stop her from loving you. I just want you to know that if the day comes when you are free from revenge and killing, I'll give you a job on my ranch. A job that'll keep you out of saloons, away from poker games, and one that will make Elizabeth happy."

"What about my happiness, Sam?" I asked. "Do you want to control my life or make Elizabeth happy?"

"I can't control your life, Charles. I can hardly control my own. Although I've always been a God fearing Christian man, I haven't always walked the straight and narrow. I guess we'll just have to ask the Lord to guide us. Both of us. Will you agree to that much?"

"I haven't seen the inside of a church since my folks were buried, Sam. God didn't leave me much when he took them. I can't ask much from Him."

"He doesn't ask for much from you, Charles. All he asks is that you forgive others and he'll forgive you."

"I'll come to that part when I get there, I reckon, Sam."

"OK, Charles," he said, and struggled to get up on his crutches. I offered to help by extending a hand.

"I'll manage," was all he said, and hobbled across the room, opened the door and was gone, leaving me standing there wondering if he had told me that he would bless my proposal to Elizabeth, or that he'd turn his back and let fate play it out.

He was right about God.

Whatever might happen would all be in God's hands, and that's the way I felt about it.

CHAPTER 35

I stood there looking at the door for a few minutes, thinking about what Sam had said. He had told me that Elizabeth loved me. That thought alone was ringing bells in my head. I felt giddy and unsure of what I was going to do next.

I sat on the bed and thought about what might have caused Elizabeth to confide in her Dad about her feelings for me. I couldn't think of anything that I had told her or that she had said to me that might have been the reason. It was just my nature to wonder about things like that.

I suddenly wanted to see her more than anything in the world.

I left my room and went to the lobby. The old lady was at the counter and I asked her if Miss McAllister had returned to her room. She didn't say anything, she just pointed behind me towards the stairs and I turned and looked.

There stood Elizabeth. She was wearing the dress I had purchased and left at the general store for her. She was so beautiful I thought I might faint. Her hair was done up and she wore a ribbon in it that was the same color as the dress. Her eyes sparkled like stars.

I took a few hesitant steps towards her, not knowing what to say or what to do. I figured I'd just take her in my arms and kiss her, but then that might not be the proper thing to do, and I wanted everything to be proper with Elizabeth.

"Hello, Charles," she said. "My, don't you look alarmed. Are you afraid of me?"

"I just didn't expect to see you so soon, Elizabeth," I stammered. "It's so good to see you again."

"I love this dress, Charles," she said, twirling around on her heels, holding her arms straight out and letting the dress billow away from her. She stopped twirling and looked at me.

"Do you like it, Charles? Thank you for it. I was hesitant to take it, but Dad said it was OK. Whatever made you buy me a dress, and how did you know my size?"

"How'd you happen to get that dress? I told the storekeeper to give it to you after a year if I didn't come back for it."

We had been standing ten feet apart and she took dainty steps towards me, took my hands in hers and smiled.

"Don't be angry at him, Charles," she said. "I was shopping in his store and I accidentally saw the package with the note on it. I made him give it to me."

I stood there silently and admired her. She was beautiful. How could I be mad at the storekeeper?

"I'll wear it to the dance tonight," she said. "Of course I'll only wear it if you are going to be there."

"I'd be pleased to, Elizabeth," I said. "But I haven't heard anything about a dance. Where's there a dance?"

"The Carrillo family is having a dance in honor of Senator Barstow. It will be at their hacienda about two miles south of town."

"I'll be there," I said. Then hastily I followed up with, "Unless, of course, you would like for me to escort you to the dance."

"No," she said.   "Dad and I will go out in the buckboard. I will save the first dance for you, though."

"Then I'll see you this evening, Elizabeth," I said, bowing. I would have kissed her hand but I knew the old lady at the counter was watching.

I tipped my hat as I walked past her and out the door. For now, I wanted to talk to Skinny Horse about an Apache named River Mouth.

CHAPTER 36

It turns out that River Mouth was a half-breed Apache, his mother was Spanish, his father an Apache that had long since decided that the ways of the White Men were going to be an easier life than the grueling survival of the desert.

Skinny Horse was glad to see me and told me all about the man I was looking for, the one called River Mouth because he never stopped talking.

"His mouth is like deep river," Skinny Horse explained. "It flows forever. Talk, talk, talk. Never quiet."

"Does he speak in Apache tongue, Spanish, or like me?"

"He speak all. Ways of Apache, ways of the rich Carrillo and like you, cowboy."

"Where can I find him?"

"You go to dance? I see you have clean shirt today."

"Oh, well I just cleaned up a little to see Elizabeth, but yes, she invited me to go to the dance. Will I be able to talk to River Mouth there?"

"If he is quiet enough to listen," he said.

"Are you going?"

"Doc ask me same thing. I would like to go very much. Young lady from rich family is nice to me, I see her at general store, she smile and I say, 'Hello pretty woman,' and she say, hello but like rich family talk. 'Boonass

Deeass.' I don't know what it mean, Doc tell me it mean hello."

I laughed at his tale and soon we were pointing at each other and slapping our thighs and roaring with laughter. Doc stepped out of his office and yelled at us.

"You two heathens quiet down, I'm trying to listen to a baby's heartbeat through the mother's stomach, and all I can hear is two jackasses braying!"

"Hi Doc," I said, choking back my laughter.

"Hello Charles Merritt. How's the deputy doing?"

"I'm surviving, Doc." I said. "Have you learned anything further about that blood stain?"

"No doubt it is human blood," he said. "I'll testify to that at your train robbing trial and at the trial for Blacky. I hope they hang the bastard."

"My friend wants to go to the dance tonight, Doc. Are you up to letting him go?"

"I told him he could go!" Doc said adamantly. "If he wants to learn to speak Spanish, that would be the first stop for him."

"I know Spanish," Skinny Horse said. "Boonass Deeass!"

Doc started laughing at that and I started with just a giggle till Skinny Horse roared, then we were back to pointing at each other like a couple of monkeys, slapping our thighs, then pointing at the Doc and laughing louder.

Doc stopped laughing suddenly and yelled.

"Shut it up!"

We calmed down.

Doc turned and walked back into his office where the expecting mother probably thought there was an idiot convention going on outside.

CHAPTER 37

By six o:clock I was thinking I'd never get to the Carrillo ranch. The directions that Doc had given me were beginning to create doubts in my mind. Maybe Doc had been drinking too much of that snake oil when he drove his buckboard out to the Carrillo's last.

He told me that there was a rocky outcropping ledge that I'd ride between and that when I got through it I would go around to the right and would see the buildings of the ranch from there. I guess I hadn't gone quite for enough to see it, but then I was still so danged tired I wanted to rein in Paint, dismount and take a nap. The thought of seeing Elizabeth again kept me in the saddle. I rode another fifty yards and there was another twenty foot high rock ledge on my right. I kicked Paint gently in the ribs with my knees and he loped ahead until I could see to my right around the rocks.

There they were, the ranch buildings. It was just about twilight and the hacienda was lit up. I could see several buckboards and a few horses tied to a rail outside the front wall of the place. The stucco wall was nearly as high as Paint's head, and when we reached it, I swung down and threw the reins around the rail a few times. Paint settled down immediately and I walked towards an opening in the wall. I could hear muffled voices and the faint sounds of a guitar somewhere in the distance.

Once inside the wall, voices grew a little louder. One voice I recognized immediately was Sam McAllister's.

He was talking in a loud voice to a tall, olive complexioned man dressed in a tight fitting suit of black shiny material with silver buttons. His graying hair stuck out in places from beneath a large black sombrero.

Sam saw me coming and hollered at me.

"Charles Merritt!" He said. "Glad you could make it, come and meet my friend Carlos Carrillo. Carlos, this is Charles Merritt, the young man I was telling you about."

I took off my hat and held out my hand. Carrillo shook my hand and smiled, but I noticed he didn't doff his hat. Either bad manners or a good custom, I thought.

"Buenos tardes, Charles." He said, smiling. "I am pleased to meet you. Sam was telling me that you are working on the disappearance of cattle on nearby ranches. I have lost a lot in the past year."

His English was perfect, and I wondered briefly if he had studied at an English university.

"Well, sir, I've did some tracking," I said. "Can't say as how I've found anything definite, but I'm working on it."

"Bueno!" He said. I knew that meant "good" so I didn't respond. Sam said something but I wasn't paying attention, I was looking around trying to spot Elizabeth. Through an opened arched doorway I saw her. My heart raced a little. She was talking to a beautiful girl, tall and slim, who looked a lot like Carlos Carrillo.

"Excuse me," I muttered and walked towards the house.

Inside I took off my hat and stood near the door. Elizabeth saw me and I thought I could see her eyes light up a little. My heart was pounding by now. I'd never seen any girls as beautiful as the two who were standing there.

"Charles," Elizabeth said. "I'd like you to meet Consuela Carrillo."

"How'd you do, Ma'am." I said, as politely as I could.

Consuela looked at me and smiled. Her teeth were like brightly polished pearls. If I hadn't already fallen head over heels in love with Elizabeth, I'd have been smitten for sure by her beauty.

"Ola', Charles," she said. "Welcome to our humble hacienda."

She spoke very good English, too, and I was curious about how the Mexican people had managed to master English so easily when it was very difficult for Americans to learn to speak Spanish.

We chatted for a few minutes, and I guess I began to let my mind drift a bit. I wasn't too much interested in how the hacienda was decorated, or the food that would be served in the patio, or the flowers. What I wanted to do was spend some alone time with Elizabeth.

It was right about then when I heard the pounding of hooves from near the wall outside, and a man hollering something that sounded like "jailbreak" but I wasn't sure. I excused myself and half ran back to the wall where a group of five or six men had collected, surrounding a horse and rider.

I could hear better outside and caught the next few words.

"How in the hell can that happen?" It was Sam McAllister.

"Well, the back wall of the cell just crumbled, sir. It made such a noise it scared the daylights out of me and when the dust settled enough I ran out there. Blacky was mounting a horse and three other riders were undoing ropes from the cell window bars. Then they rode off."

The speaker was young Ted Bradshaw. When he saw me, he turned and looked directly in my face.

"I'm sorry, deputy," he said. "Wasn't much I could do but watch them three untie their ropes, mount up and ride a way."

"No one's blaming you, Ted." I said. "Do you know who any of the men were? Ever seen 'em before?"

"I can't say," he said. "There was still a lot of dust floating around and I couldn't see their faces real good."

"Give my regrets to Elizabeth, Sam," I said, unhitching Paint's reins from the rail.

"Where you going" he asked.

"I'm going to get Blacky. I'll track them. Any of you other men want to ride a posse, mount up."

"I go," I heard a voice and turned. It was Skinny Horse.

"No, you stay and learn medicine." I said. "Doc may need you more than I will.. If you'd care to ride with me, Mr. Carrillo, I'd be happy to have you."

"I can't leave my guests, Charles, but I'll send some men to meet you in town. They will be at your disposal."

"Thank you, sir." I said, and mounted.

Tired as I was, I felt I owed it to Garrett for trusting me enough to deputize me. Now I had to ride.

As I rode towards town I looked around and found that there were only two other men with me. Big posse, I thought. But then Carrillo had promised to send some men to town to ride with me. I didn't push Paint too hard. There didn't seem to be a reason to ride hard back to town just to look at a crumbled jail wall. I knew that Blacky would have at least a four hour head start on me, but with luck I'd be able to pick up his trail out of town, and I'd follow it until I caught him. The way it looked now, Blacky was the man who'd shot Bradshaw and I felt that somehow connected with trying to keep me from returning the railroad's money.

My biggest regret was that I had missed my good chance to get Elisabeth off to ourselves and talk about what her daddy had told me.

CHAPTER 38

There were still some town folks standing in back of the jail, milling around, pointing, and yakking. I recognized the young bartender and the store keeper as well as a few cowboys who'd been in card games I'd played.

I didn't waste any time.

"Anyone want to ride with me to catch the man who just broke out of here?"

No one answered. I looked around, shook my head and turned to the two who had ridden in with me. Carrillo's men hadn't shown up.

"Well I guess it's just us, then," I said. "Let's ride."

It was nearly dark but we rode out, stopping occasionally to make sure we were headed in the same general direction as the escape party. A full moon helped us keep an eye on the tracks we were following. We didn't ride fast, just steady. Paint was well rested and eager to lope but I reined him back to a fast walk. There were too many pitfalls a horse could get into while running fast in the dark. I was aware that the men ahead of us somewhere would be subject to the same dangers as we faced, trying to ride too far, too fast. I figured they would be keeping a pace not much faster than ours.

As I rode I tried to think of what I would do if I were Blacky. The tracks were headed due south, and I thought that Blacky would head for the border. Whoever broke him out of jail would have been prepared to ride for a long way before stopping. That meant they had water, food and fresh horses. Our horses were fresh but in our haste to get on the trail of the escape party we had neglected to check our water supply. I felt for the canteen looped over the saddle horn and shook it. It felt like it was about half full. Too late now, I thought.

The moon lit up the desert like someone was holding a powerful lantern above us. There were no sounds except the thudding of hooves as we rode, and no other life that we could see ahead of us. Once, a jackrabbit broke and ran away from the trail, spooked Paint a bit, and I had to grip his neck with my knees and pat him a little to get him settled down.

I got drowsy after an hour of riding and let myself drift into a half awake stage, catching bits of sleep. My two companions were talking to each other, most of their conversation had to do with women and poker so I wasn't listening. In the moments that I rested I thought of Elizabeth. Was her daddy right? Should I give up being a deputy and settle down to a routine job of ranching? Should I forsake my dream of owning my own spread to go to work for her daddy? Something in my heart told me that I probably wouldn't be happy riding for someone else's ranch, but something else told me that whatever it took to be Elizabeth's husband, is what I would gladly do.

The big question wasn't about the kind of work I'd be doing, though. The main thing was whether I'd be willing to let Will's killer go, or shoot him down in some dusty street somewhere. Not one time had it ever occurred to me that I wouldn't be the man to walk away from a gunfight involving Will's killer. I had seen it in my mind's eye a hundred times.

We'd face each other twenty feet apart. I'd watch his midsection like my Daddy had taught me to do. I'd know when he made his move because something would twitch. I'd pull the Colt and point as soon as the barrel cleared my holster. I'd be pulling the trigger, not once, but as many times as it took.

He might get off a shot, but all of my shots would hit him. If he hit me, it wouldn't stop me from throwing lead at him. My will power against Will's killer was the way I thought of it.

Suddenly a thought crept into my head. Would Will have survived the train ride to Tucson? Would he have died if he hadn't been shot in the chest under that water tank? Would the man that shot Will have wasted lead? I knew that Will had been near death. There was nothing I could have done to save him. I'd heard of men having a doctor open up their guts and taking an appendix out and then sewing them back up only to have them die from infection a few days later.

Did that polecat that shot Will just hasten the inevitable fact that Will's death was imminent? That thought made me think of my own mortality. I'd been near death on more than one occasion. Whatever had kept me from getting the smallpox that killed my folks was something I'd thought about often. And the infection that had eaten away at my leg before Will had got me to that hospital in Tennessee might just have well laid me low.

Then there was the incident where Roper had tried to gun me down and I had turned my head in his direction just in time to see him point his gun at me.

The way I figured it, there was a power somewhere that had it all planned out. I was alive, Will was dead. He'd been a brother to me, and I knew that if it meant losing Elizabeth, losing my own life, or losing my eternal salvation, the man that killed Will was going to die the same way Will died, with a ball of lead ripping through his heart.

Somewhere in the darkness I heard the sound of pounding hoofs, riding hard. It was just starting to break daylight and I awoke fast from the slumber and dreams that had came to me as I rocked back and forth in the saddle.

I looked all around and from behind us I saw a small cloud of dust. Whoever it was had intent on catching up with us so I waited, thinking it might be Carrillo's men that he had promised. Through the early morning light I could see that it was two riders. When they got closer, I recognized one of them. It was Dressler.

"D'ya mind if I ride with you?" he said as he reined in his horse near mine.

"Glad to have you," I said. "Who's that you've got with you?"

"Name's River Mouth," he said.

So that's the man that I was told about. Chester Peak said he was with the Indians who sold stolen cattle. I wondered why he had suddenly switched allegiance and decided to go after a jail breaking killer.

"You speak English?" I asked the short, heavy set rider.

"Uno poquito," A little bit.

"You sold cattle to a railroad conductor named Peak?"

"I help round up cattle. Drive them south to iron horse track. Man named Black sell them."

"That's what he told me," Dressler said. "How far ahead do you reckon Blacky is?"

"I figure we'll catch up with them early in the morning if we ride most of the night."

"Good." Dressler said.

"What's your hand in all of this, Dressler?"

"I've got my own reasons," he said. "Don't ask me any questions and I'll tell you no lies."

We were riding at an easy trot as we talked, our shadows stretched long in the sand in front of us. The breaking light made it seem as though we were always riding into darkness. Ahead I saw a narrowing of the trail we were on, dark cliffs on either side.

I had more questions I wanted to ask of River Mouth, and he seemed willing to talk, but the study drum of horses hooves made it nearly impossible to carry on a conversation, so I figured I'd wait to finish my inquiry.

The terrain ahead was similar to that area I'd ridden through just before getting to the Carrillo ranch, rock outcroppings that started no taller than my knees, and gradually got larger until some were as high as my horse's shoulders, some taller. I looked ahead and saw that we would pass through a straight where the rocks were thirty or forty feet higher than my horse.

I instinctively slowed Paint to a mere walk. Ahead of me, one of the riders suddenly lurched sideways in his saddle and I heard the crack of a rifle. I reined Paint hard to the right and guided him with my knees through an opening where the rocks were boulder size. I heard a rider coming behind me, and suddenly the gunfire commenced. Shots were resounding from nearby but a deadly volley of rounds was being fired from above and ahead of us.

Once through the opening, I pulled back on the reins and Paint stopped within a few feet. I left the saddle fast, pulling the Winchester out of its scabbard as I dropped. I scrambled to the top of the ledge in front of me and peered over, trying to pick out a silhouette on the ridge ahead. I saw nothing.

Below me I heard the sound of boots hitting the sand and glanced down. It was Dressler.

"See anything?"

"No," I said. "They've taken cover up there, and can pick us off easily if we get out in the open."

Gunfire had stopped as quickly as it had began.

"What's the plan?"

"I wish I knew," I said. "Any ideas?"

"Well, I reckon the only way to get out of this is to ride around these rocks and climb up at them from the other side."

"Might be foolhardy," I said. "They've got the advantage, looking down, and climbing might be tough."

"Tough with boots on," he said, sitting down and starting to pull his boots off.

"I'll go," I told him.

"No, I'll do it. You keep them pinned down from back here. I'll see if I can get close enough to pick some of them off. If so, wait till the shooting stops and listen for my pop gun."

He shuffled his hands and held up a derringer. It would make a small popping sound, compared to the hammering sound of a Winchester.

"You got a rifle?" I asked.

"Yep. I reckon a man can shoot further with a rifle than he can with a hand gun."

I thought about that for a second. It sounded like something Will might say.

"All right. I'll come up from this side when I hear your derringer."

"Don't take any chances," he said.

"You're taking the chances," I told him. "You don't have to do this. It ain't your dogfight."

"I'm making it my fight," he said, "Watch my boots for me, will you?" He climbed back on his horse and left his boots sitting in the sand. I heard the gentle thud of his horse's hooves slapping sand for a half a minute until they faded out. Horse and rider were hidden behind the rock outcropping.

The Winchester I was holding over the top of the ledge was getting heavy in my outstretched arm so I slid my body up and relaxed, just the crown of my hat showing above the rocks. That was enough. The hat flipped backwards a split second before I heard the crack of a rifle. I risked a glance over the top and saw muzzle smoke a hundred yards up and ahead of me on the top of the ridge on my left. I fired, cocked and fired again in the general direction of the smoke.

The pow-pow-pow of rifles from above reached my ears concurrent with the whine of slugs ricocheting off of the rock ledge. That gunfire was returned almost immediately from somewhere across the trail at the base of a ten foot boulder. One of the cowboys who had ridden out with me must have made it to those rocks but I was pretty sure the other one was dead. He had dropped like a fly after the first shot was fired.

There was a sudden silence, no one was taking wild shots. I peeked over the top and saw nothing above to warrant shooting at, and wondered how long it would take Dressler to reach the other end of the pass and climb high enough to see the ambush gang. Judging from the distance I had seen gun smoke, I figured it was about two hundred yards through the pass. At a careful walk or ambling gait, a horse will walk four miles in an hour, so a quick calculation told me that it would take about 3 minutes for Dressler's horse to walk 200 yards.

About two minutes had already passed. I'd wait another minute then open fire. That should provide enough of a detraction to let Dressler start climbing. My position against the face of the rock was too precarious to look at Grandpa's watch, so I counted off the seconds. When I reached 60 I raised my head slowly, remembering the accuracy of the shot that had sent my hat flying. With my eyes barely over the edge, I saw a movement high and almost straight across from my position. One of the jail break gang was trying to work his way towards the cowboy who was across from me in low rocks.

I could see just the shoulders and head of the man. I took careful aim and squeezed. I hit him in the chest and he stood up straight, then tumbled head over heels off of the rock ledge. My shot caused a bevy of return shots, and my posse rider cut loose with a salvo. I stuck the

Winchester over the top and fired. I had now fired five times and my rifle was empty. The remaining Winchester rounds were in Paint's saddlebags.

I slid down the face of the rock until my boots hit sand and reached for the saddlebags. I heard a quick volley of three shots, spaced almost equally apart, then silence. As I reloaded the Winchester I heard the diminutive sound of the two shot derringer. Pop. Pop.

That told me that Dressler had reached a point where he had fired at the men who had been returning my fire. I wondered how many he had taken out of the fight.

I finished loading and stuck the Winchester back in the scabbard and swung up on Paint, wheeled his head around and walked him through the passage that had brought us in to this spot. When I reached the trail, I kicked Paint in the flanks and leaned as far to the right as I could, behind Paint's neck and rode towards the far end of the pass. I drew a couple of shots from somewhere up on the ridge, then heard another shot, then silence.

A few seconds later I flew past the last of the outcropping and as I did I saw a lone rider ahead of me, fifty yards or so, his horse kicking up dust in a hasty retreat.

I reined up and yelled at the top of my lungs.

"DRESSLER."

"Yo!" I heard from above me.

"How many are left?"

"I got two," he yelled down. "You?"

"One," I said. "That leaves the one who just rode out and one more."

"You sure there were five?"

"I only counted five horses we were trailing, didn't you count?"

"Hell I couldn't tell if there was five or fifty," he said. "I don't see too well in the dark."

"You saw well enough to dispatch two of the bunch to hell!"

"The sun was shining towards me," he said. I could hear the shuffling of his trousers as he climbed back down, and his heavy breathing. "They were silhouetted. Like shooting fish in a rain barrel."

By now I could see him, making his way carefully down an almost sheer face of the rock, bare feet finding footholds and long arms easing himself down.

When he dropped the last few feet to the ground he sat down and took fine wool stockings from his pocket and started to pull them on.

"Give me my boots."

"Oh, I forgot your boots," I said. "I'll ride back and get them."

"Never mind," he told me. "Get after Blacky. That was him that's riding away. I'll go get my boots."

I didn't hesitate, spurred Paint in the direction the rider had gone, and took off. Now I was a hundred and fifty yards behind. I should have just lit out after him, and would have, had I known it was Blacky.

Paint was gaining on Blacky's horse, but I knew it was going to take a long, bone jarring ride to chase Blacky down. After a while I was sure that I had gained almost a hundred yards, but Paint was rasping his breath over the bit and I knew he was tiring.

CHAPTER 39

I had an idea. It evolved out of my first thought that Paint would never be able to catch Blacky's horse, his horse had rested for 4 hours or so and was fresh, I'd ridden Paint all night.

The idea was to use my Winchester and shoot Blacky's horse out from under him. I immediately dismissed the thought, hell, I'd rather shoot Blacky than any horse. The horse had done nothing. I was pretty sure that Blacky was the polecat that had shot Will.

The idea evolved as I pushed Paint hard, riding in the dust of Blacky's horse. Instead of shooting the horse, maybe I could shoot close enough to its feet to spook it. Just as the idea crept through the fog of fatigue in my noggin, I saw a saguaro cactus in the dimness of early morning shadows ahead of Blacky.

I reined Paint to a quick stop, yanked the Winchester out of the holster and took careful aim at an arm of the giant cactus. I held aim, holding my breath, until Blacky's horse was two and a half heads from the cactus, then squeezed, cocked the gun and fired again. The cactus arm dropped in front of the horse, and much to my relief, the plan worked.

Blacky's horse leapt almost straight up, came down hard on all fours, then skidding to a stop, it reared on its back legs. Blacky leaned forward in the saddle trying to stay on, but the motion was so fast that his hind-end slid over the cantle. When the horse's front end came down, Blacky was still sliding to one side. The horse then crow hopped with all four feet off of the ground and did a ninety degree turn in mid air. Blacky hit the ground with a grunt so loud I could hear it from where I was.

I spurred Paint into a gallop and was twenty yards away when Blacky got to his feet. He turned to face me as I reined up and dismounted on Paint's left, my horse between me and Blacky. I had caught just the first motion of Blacky's hand going for his gun. I hoped he wouldn't fire; if he fired he would hit Paint. I had to stop him.

I slapped Paint on his hind end with my right hand and jerked back hard on the reins with my left. Paint responded just like I hoped he would, he pivoted, head first and around me to my left, leaving me facing Blacky, who's gun hand had reached the grip on his revolver.

I didn't want Blacky dead. I wanted to talk to him about Will. There wasn't time to think about the shot I had to make. I'd started my draw a split second after slapping Paint on his butt, and now my hand was extracting the .44 just like I'd practiced a million times. The barrel cleared leather as my first shot cleared the end of it.

The slug found its mark, high and on Blacky's gun arm. It spun him around like a willow in the wind. His hand kept pulling on his gun and it cleared as he spun. His motion carried him down and away from the second slug that ripped away from my .44. It missed him.

He fell hard, pinning his gun arm beneath him.

"Freeze, Blacky," I yelled at the top of my lungs.

He laid there, still and not moving. I heard a horse coming from behind me and figured it must be Dressler. Instinct told me to look and I did. It wasn't Dressler, it was River Mouth.

Blacky rolled to his left, trying to free his gun arm as I ran towards him. Just as his gun hand started to lift, I kicked the gun. It went flying back and clanged off of a small boulder somewhere behind him.

"You've got about ten seconds to tell me why you shot Will if you want to live," I screamed at him.

Blacky looked at me. His eyes narrowed and he spat towards my boots. I drew back my right hand, still holding the .44. I would have laid his head open.

"Hold it!"

I turned, thinking at first it was River Mouth who had interrupted me, he was dismounted and stood there with the reins of his horse in his hands.

It wasn't him.

It was Dressler.

"You stay out of this," I said.

"No. I'll not stay out of it," Dressler said, slowly and forcefully. "He didn't shoot Will."

"How can you be so sure of that?" I asked.

"I shot Will," he said, his voice trailing off.

"You?"

I stood there looking at him. Dressler shot Will? I couldn't believe what I'd heard. My first thought is that I'd not heard it at all, then I thought that Dressler just didn't want me to face a jury for killing Blacky. Confusion crept up my back like a scorpion.

"What are you telling me, Dressler?"

"Put your gun away, Charles, and I'll finish."

"I'll put it away," I said. "But when you're through talking you better start drawing, cause I am going to kill you."

"I won't draw," he said. "I shot Will, and if you ever listened to anyone in your life, Charles, listen to me."

"Go ahead."

"I wasn't on that train that day by accident," he started. "It was just fate that you brought Will on and sat him down across from me. He was the main reason I'd come west."

"What's that supposed to mean?" I asked.

"I'm not who you think I am," Dressler said.

"I don't know much about you, Dressler," I said. "I know you're a gunfighter, you've got a reputation. That won't stop me from killing you if you're telling me the truth."

"I said I won't draw on you," he said, slowly moving his hands to his belt buckle. He undid it. The silver handled .45 in its holster pulled the belt lose and it dropped to the ground.

"Watch my hands closely now," he said. I watched.

He moved his hands down and away from his body. A double barreled derringer dropped from each of his hands, I hadn't even seen them reach his hands. They must have dropped out of his sleeves.

"That's it," he said. "I'm unarmed. You wouldn't shoot an unarmed man, would you?"

"Talk," I said.

"Would a man kill his own son, Charles?"

"I wouldn't think so," I said. "Keep talking."

"Well that's exactly what happened. You see, I'm Will's father," he said, sadly, shaking his head slowly back and forth as if he could erase the thought by doing so.

"Will's your son? You killed Will? By accident?"

"No, it wasn't an accident, I pulled the trigger knowing he would die. Pain is an intimidating, grinding enemy to a man, Charles. It will make men insane."

"Will was in a lot of pain. He begged me to shoot him to stop that pain. He thought that I was you. First, he begged me to get him off of the train. That was a mile or so before we got to the water tank. The train had started to slow down and the conductor said we would be stopping for water. I don't remember his words, but it was something like 'I don't want to die on this damned train to the sun, I just want to die on the ground.'"

He stood there for a few seconds still looking at the ground. What he had told me was buzzing through my mind like the bullets had ricocheted off of the rocks a mile or so back. I was trying desperately to understand what he was telling me, but it wasn't making sense.

"Let me start a ways back, Charles." Dressler finally spoke, looking at me with his steel gray eyes.

"I've been looking for Will for nearly ten years. I knew he'd been in the war, and I traced him to your place in Kentucky. I don't know how much of Will's past he told you, but his mother took him and went back to Virginia when Will was a boy. Tennessee wasn't kind to her, we'd lost our little girl when Will was two, and after that Will's mother wasn't the same. I left and traveled to California to look for gold."

"Will's momma stayed in Virginia for a couple of years then went back to Tennessee looking for me. She got sick soon after and died leaving Will with her brother. I got tied up in California and by the time I got back to

Tennessee the war between the States was over and Will was gone."

"Will was raised by that Uncle?" I asked.

"If you can call it that," he said. "I learned from neighbors that he mistreated Will. Eventually I had to kill him when he turned on me. I served a year in the pen for killing him, even though he'd drawn on me. The jury was sympathetic towards him because he only had one arm.

"After I got out of prison a cousin of his called me a coward and forced me into a gunfight. I had to kill him. That's when I started to get the reputation of a gunslinger."

"Will's name wasn't Dressler," I said. "It was Durant."

"That was his mother's name when I married her," he said, and left it at that.

I had started to understand what he was telling me. It was soaking into my noggin like a fog.

"In Abilene I picked up your trail again. It was about that time I ran out of money and had to take a job. Local ranchers had formed an association and they hired me. Here's the real coincidence, Charles. The Free Range Association hired me as a detective. I worked finding two-bit cattle rustlers."

"When an opportunity presented itself to move to Phoenix and work for the Association, I jumped at the chance. I figured I could search for Will and work at the same time. So you and I are after the same men, Charles."

"Why were you on that train, and how'd you know Will was your son?"

"I'll get to the train later," he said. "I would have never recognized Will. It was you that I recognized when you brought him aboard. I had found pictures of you at your folks house in Kentucky. I asked neighbors and they told me how you and Will had tried to run a store, worked in the mines, and finally headed west. I followed. I recognized you from those pictures, and when you called the man you brought on the train, Will, I almost passed out. I'd found my son and he was dying."

"You haven't told me why you shot Will." I said.

"I got Will off of the train at the water tank. I laid him down in the shade and he was shivering all over like he had malaria. He opened his eyes and looked at me and spoke."

"Charlie, I can't make it." He said. "Here's where I get off, buddy. We've had a good ride, but I'm dying. I want you to shoot me, Charlie. I've suffered enough and I won't live to get to Tucson. Leave me here in the shade and go on back to the spread. But don't leave me alive, Charlie, the critters will eat me. Just do it. I'd do the same for you."

CHAPTER 40

Blacky had just laid there listening to all of the story, now he spoke.

"Why don't you two quit gabbing and patch me up?"

I turned to River Mouth and told him to catch Blacky's horse. I tied a bandana around Blacky's arm and poured whiskey on it from a bottle I had in my saddlebags.

"Give me a drink of that," he said.

"Shut up, Blacky," I said. "I wanted to shoot you for killing Will, and I might still shoot you for killing Bradshaw, you think I'm going to give you my whiskey to drink?"

I turned back to Dressler and saw that he had turned his back on me and was sobbing, his broad shoulders heaving. I went to him.

"Here," I said. I touched the bottle to his arm. He took it and raised it to his lips and drank.

"You still want to shoot me, cowboy?" He asked, his deep voice trembling

"No."

"What would you have done, Charlie?"

"I don't know," I said truthfully.

Hoof beats interrupted us and I looked up to see River Mouth holding the reins of Blacky's horse. It had got quite a bit lighter and there was something familiar about that horse. I walked towards it and suddenly realized why it looked familiar.

It was the roan horse I'd broke at McAllister's ranch. The one I'd fought for with Younger.

I questioned Blacky about it but he wouldn't talk. We caught another saddled horse that had shied around the base of the rocks, loaded Blacky on it and started back to town. When we reached a trail that led towards the McAllister ranch, I stopped.

"If you don't mind, Dressler, would you take Blacky on in to town? I've got a bone to pick with the man who claims to own this roan."

"I'll do it if you promise you won't shoot anybody," he said. "I'd hate to see you go to jail, now that you're about to clear your reputation."

"Don't worry, I won't shoot anyone," I said. "I want McAllister to know that Younger may not be as good of a hand as he claims to be."

"Are you sure you want to convince McAllister of that, or his daughter?"

"Both" I said, grinning.

We parted company, I headed towards McAllister's and River Mouth followed Dressler and Blacky, back towards Tucson.

I was disappointed when I arrived at McAllister's ranch to find that Younger wasn't there, I really wanted to know why Blacky had been riding that roan horse. I was glad, however, to find that Sam and Elizabeth had made it back home.

"I'm glad you caught that outlaw," Sam said, after I told him what had happened at the rock outcropping.

Elizabeth was silent.

I was invited by Sam to have their evening meal with them, and accepted gratefully. Elizabeth remained quiet through the meal, polite, but quiet. It puzzled me.

I slept in the bunkhouse that night and early the next morning, knocked on the kitchen door. A lamp was on in the kitchen, and I knew that Elizabeth was up preparing breakfast for her father.

She came to the door.

"I'm going to ride back to Tucson this morning," I said, "I'll get an early start while it is cool."

"Bye, Charles," she said, as cool as the morning.

"What is it, Elizabeth?" I asked. "I don't understand why you seem to be avoiding me. You're awfully quiet."

"You don't understand anything, Charles Merritt!" she said. "You left the party before it even began, you ran off into the night looking for an escaped criminal, even though you're only a deputy, and Garrett hadn't asked you to do so. Are you not concerned about your own safety? And if you're not, why should I be."

She closed the door and I stood there for a minute with my hat in my hand. She was right. I had put myself and the two cowboys who rode with me at risk, when really it was Garrett's job to go after Blacky. I had thought at the time that I would get a clue as to who killed Will. I was right.

I'd found out who killed Will, but what I'd learned was not what I wanted deep down inside to know. I guess I had revenge implanted so deep that I didn't recognize the real reason I'd taken off after Blacky. Now I had Elizabeth upset, and that was the last thing I wanted to do.

Back in Tucson I was greeted as a hero. Everyone wanted to buy me a drink at the saloon, and I let most of them. The next morning I felt like I'd slept under a stampede, and was feeling sorry for myself about Elizabeth, when I saw Doc and Skinny Horse at the hotel's diner.

"Congratulations, Merritt, you seem to be a hero around here. Even Garrett admits you deserve accolades."

"Garret's back?"

"Yes, he's back. Have you forgotten what today is?"

"What is it?" I asked, "Someone's birthday? A hanging?"

"No, you dumb cowpoke," Doc said. "It's your trial day. Either you'll be freed or you'll go back to jail for train robbery."

"Oh, no," I said. "I had forgotten all about that. And I feel like I've been shot at and missed and shit at and hit."

"Well, you've got an hour and a half to clean up," Doc said. "Trial time is 10;30."

I gulped down my food, swallowed a cup of hot, black coffee and headed back to my room. I needed a bath but didn't have time for one. I cleaned up as best as I could, shaved, cut my long hair with my razor and put on the only clean shirt I had. I looked at myself in the mirror and really didn't like what I saw.

Outside the window on the street below I noticed people starting to gather around the saloon for my trial. I figured if I went down there now I could get a little hair of the dog that bit me before trial time. I headed for the saloon.

Dressler saw me coming out of the hotel and motioned for me. I met him in the middle of the dusty road and he asked me what I'd done at McAllister's.

"Nothing to speak of," I said. "All I accomplished was to get Elizabeth ticked off at me somehow."

"I thought that might be a problem," he said.

"What's that mean?" I asked.

"Oh, nothing. Just a thought I had," he said, and I let it go at that.

We got to the bar and the young bartender set a bottle in front of us.

"This one is on me, Merritt," he said. "Good work chasing down that jail breaker and his mob."

"Dressler did most of the hard stuff," I said.

"Don't be telling that, Charles," Dressler said.

We downed our whiskey and when the young bartender started to pour another I waved him off.

"Pour Dressler's. I've got to be awake for this trial."

CHAPTER 41

I was acquitted of train robbery. The money that had been found in the bag Blacky had drunkenly brought into the saloon was proven to be the same money from the train. The railroad pay clerk had written down numbers from the bills and those numbers matched numbers on the money. Doc's testimony convinced the jury that Blacky shot Bradshaw, since bloodstains on the bag matched bloodstains on Bradshaw's shirt.

The judge ordered that the money be given to the representative from the railroad, including my money that I had in that bag. I protested, but it didn't matter. It was considered "court expenses" and I was just out.

I quit my job as deputy and went back to ranching at McAllister's. Elizabeth forgave me and we went to a dance together shortly afterward and that was when I kissed her for the first time. Her kisses were sweeter than cinnamon buns.

It has now been 15 years since Will was shot. Blacky was tried and hanged for the murder of Bradshaw.

I married Elizabeth McAllister and headed up her father's spread for five years under the tutelage of Jim, the foreman. Then Sam McAllister, my father-in-law, died in his sleep one Sunday night.

After Sam died, I told Elizabeth that I just wasn't cut out to run a ranch and that I really wasn't happy doing so; the memory of Will and how we'd dreamed of owning a ranch ruined it all for me.

She told me that wherever I went she wanted to be, and that if I still had an itch to go to California, she'd sell the ranch and go with me. We sold the ranch to Jim and some of the other cowpokes, and taking our young son, Will, we boarded the west bound train to the sun.

I bought a place near a sprawling Mexican town called San Diego and we started raising a really strange looking fruit called 'avocado' by the Mexicans, and 'alligator pears' by the settlers that had swarmed to the southern California where it was warm and land was cheap.

One day I was shopping with Elizabeth in town, our son, Will, being accompanied by a young Mexican girl, highly recommended by a good friend of mine, Skinny Horse. He had married Elizabeth's friend, Consuela, the wealthy daughter of Carlos Carrillo.

Now he was a practicing doctor in San Diego, went by the name of Caballo, owned a hotel and a fine two story building where he had his office. He spoke good English, and excellent Spanish. I don't think I ever heard him say 'boonass dee ass' again.

As we shopped that day, a young boy stopped me and called me Senor Merritt. There was a man in the saloon who wanted to talk to me. He'd given the boy a dime to find me.

"Excuse me, Elizabeth," I said. "A man awaits me in the saloon, do you mind if I speak to him for a few minutes?"

"It isn't trouble, is it, Charles?" she asked.

"No, I don't think so, maybe a market owner." I said. "I'll tell you all about it later."

"I'll be at Doctor Caballo's office," she said. "I'll visit with them and wait for you."

I left her there and walked the short distance back to the saloon.

As I walked through the door I noticed a man dressed in fine clothes sitting at the bar with his back to me. He was watching me in the mirror behind the bar.

It was Dressler.

After a warm greeting and a couple of shots of Charter Oak while talking about old times, Dressler looked at me and suddenly his mood changed.

"Charles, I have to get this off of my chest before it's too late. I really hate to tell you this now, nearly fifteen years after you and I chased Blacky down. But after talking to Doc and Pat Garrett, I reckon they have the right idea, that the truth is always better than a lie, no matter how long it takes to come out."

"What truth are you talking about, Dressler?"

He sighed deeply and poured himself another shot from the bottle. I declined when he motioned the bottle towards me.

"Here is the truth. I did *NOT* shoot Will."

I was stunned.

He sat there silently while I thought about what he had just told me. I knew he was waiting for me to comment, but I couldn't think of anything to say. It had been such a long time, my emotions were jumbled.

"Oh, I know, I did a commendable job of convincing you that I did, and I had a good reason. Actually, a thousand good reasons. You see, Charles, Sam

McAllister paid me a thousand dollars to convince you that I was the one that shot Will."

Suddenly what he was saying started to make some sense. I remembered McAllister's visit to me in the hotel room the day of the Carrillo's party.

"Part of what I told you was true," Dressler was saying. "I am Will's father. Would a father shoot his own son? Not me, I didn't shoot Will."

"Go on," I said, holding back emotion, a tight feeling developing in my throat. I tossed down another shot to ease the pain.

"McAllister read you right, son. You would have gunned down anyone else. I don't know what kept you from shooting me after I told you that lie. I guess you felt sorry for me. When I cried, the tears were real. I was finally grieving for Will."

"Why'd you wait to tell me? You came all the way from Tucson just to tell me this?"

"Why have I waited so long? Because I think you are mature enough now to handle the truth. And, as McAllister predicted, I became a gunslinger for the second time in my life."

"I didn't tell you who shot Will. You have a right to know. It was Younger. When I rode back that night with River Mouth he told me all about it. Younger was in cahoots with Blacky. He led the bunch that pulled the wall down and let Blacky out of jail, but made the mistake of riding the roan and had it staked out the night they ambushed us. Blacky grabbed the first horse he came to. Younger was hid out in some rocks like the coward he was, and had to walk back to town, after we found Blacky's horse."

"Back to the day Will died." he said, his eyes getting misty.

"Will got off of the train under his own power. When he walked away from where you put him he said that he was sick and was getting off to puke."

"Chester lied to you about me helping Will get off, and I used that lie to convince you that I was the one who shot Will. By the way, Chester went to prison for his part in that. River Mouth told me that Younger and his bunch were selling stolen cattle to Chester Peak that day. Younger was close enough to be seen by Will, and he put a slug in Will to keep him from talking."

"When I confronted him about all of that, he threw down on me, and I killed him. Garrett witnessed that gunfight so I didn't have to stand trial for it."

"Eventually it had to happen though. One night I was playing poker in the saloon where we used to play. A cowboy wanted to make a name for his self. I had to kill him. Witnesses said I drew first, and I did. He hadn't even touched his gun handle when I shot."

"I just finished a five year sentence for manslaughter. The second time I've lost a part of my life."

That shocked me. I glanced at his face and saw nothing there but resolution to start a new life, leave the gunslinger image behind him. That image would have been mine had I killed Younger.

"So now you know."

"What are your plans?" I asked.

"I figured I'd go up to San Francisco. I know some people there, if they're still living. Maybe change my name and find some nice woman and settle down."

Outside the saloon I could hear the sound of a steam engine starting. The train station was right around the corner. The train wouldn't be headed into the sun, but north to the thriving metropolis of San Francisco.

Dressler stood up and stuck out his hand. I shook it.

"Good bye, Charles Merritt. My regards to Elizabeth, and if you're ever in San Francisco, look me up."

"So long Dressler," I said. "And thank you."

"Don't mention it," he said, and in two or three long strides, gliding like he had that day so long ago in the saloon in Tucson, he was gone.

THE END.

About the author:

Don Yarber is better known for his Kip Yardley, PI series, Bodies and Beaches, Corpses and Canyons, Death and Deep Waters, and Evil and Everglades. He ventured away from the PI novel to write The Sign Killer, and now has tried his hand at an entirely different genre, the Western Novel.

He lives near Morganfield, Kentucky with his wife, Shirley, and his dog, Blondie, and two cats, Smokey and Wiggly.